Jea

By

Eve Langlais

Book Two in the Freakn' Shifters Series

Copyright © November 2011, Eve Langlais
Cover Art by Amanda Kelsey © November 2011
Edited by Brieanna Robertson
Produced in Canada

Published by Eve Langlais
Suite 126 — 2377 Hwy #2 Unit 120
Bowmanville ON, L1C 5E2
www.EveLanglais.com

ISBN-13: 978-1467957526

ISBN-10: 1467957526

Jealous And Freakn' – Eve Langlais

How can she make him stop thinking of her as a freakn' sister?

Francine's loved Mitchell, a wolf like herself, since she first set eyes on him back when they were just kids. However, Mitchell's never seen her as more than another annoying sister. Determined to make him realize she's all grown up, she enlists the aide of Alejandro, a gorgeous cat shifter. She never counted on wanting them both.

Alejandro knows Francine is special from the first moment he meets the fiery plump wolf, which is why he suggests she use him to make Mitchell jealous. A great plan, especially if it means he gets to kiss those luscious lips. One taste, though, and he's addicted, but how does he make her see past the man she loves to realize she's also meant to be his mate?

For a long time now, Mitchell's been avoiding Francine, his bratty sister's friend. However, the little girl he remembers is all grown up, and when he sees her in the arms of another, a need to claim her overrides all his common sense. But, he's waited too long and fate has decided that he's going to have to share. Can he bend enough to accept Francine with her other man, or will his freakn' jealousy send him running?

Warning: Excessive amounts of heat may be generated when reading this story. Do not sit or stand near flammable objects unless they happen to be your partner. Please note that while the heroes sustained injuries during the course of the story, Francine did eventually kiss them all better, naked of course. This is a ménage romance, with heavy emphasis on the romance. It does contain multi-partner, sexual situations that some people may find titillating. Reader discretion is advised.

Acknowledgements

Hubby, as usual, gets a thank you for being my inspiration and biggest fan. Love you, George.

I'd also like to extend a great, big thank you to Brandie Buckwine, a fellow author, who Beta read this piece for me. Not only did she spot some pesky typos, but with her advice, helped me make one scene super special. You rock!

Prologue

Legs pumping wildly, he tore through the woods behind his house, unfortunately too far from the shelter of his room. Despite his speed, he knew his pursuer owned fleeter feet—and unwavering determination. If he were to survive, he needed to hide, and quickly. Panting, he stopped and perused the area. Eyes frantically scanning, he searched for somewhere to hide. He said a short prayer begging the ground to open up and swallow him. No such luck.

The rustling sound of his stalker approached, and panic gripped him. He couldn't allow himself to get caught, not after what happened last time. He thought about wiggling his skinny body under the partially collapsed tree, however the idea of becoming trapped halted him. Perhaps he could climb a tree? Cover himself in leaves? Or…

Too late. A hundred pounds of persistence tackled him to the ground, knocking the breath from him. Before he could wiggle free, the bane of his existence grabbed his arms and pinned him.

"Gotcha!" Bright brown eyes set in a freckled face with a gap-toothed smile stared down at him.

Dammit, she'd caught him, again. At least this time his brothers and friends weren't around to ridicule him.

"Francine," he said, trying to sound stern like his mother, not an easy thing to do with a thirteen-year-old voice prone to cracking. "Let me go."

"Not 'til you say it," she ordered with the command of a queen stifled in a ten-year-old's body.

"No. I won't." To admit it would probably cause the end of the world, his world, not to mention make him a laughing stock.

"Oh yes you will," she said with a grin, leaning close, the aroma of watermelon bubble gum wafting over him. "I'm not letting you go until you do."

And she wouldn't. Francine owned a few pounds on his yet to grow frame. This was one of the times his runt status sucked. "Don't make me hurt you," he warned, even if he didn't actually mean it. His mother would kill him if he bent a hair on Francine's head, his baby sister's best friend and ultimate pain in his ass.

"Ha. I'd like to see you try. We both know I could kick your butt in a second. Now tell me."

"No."

She retaliated, her fingers letting go of him only to dig under his arms, going straight for his ticklish spots. Mitchell screamed and squirmed as she tortured him, but he couldn't manage to push her off, no matter how much he tried.

"Say it!"

"Never!"

She gave him a purple nurple, twisting his nipple until he let out an ungodly squeal that no animal or boy should make.

"Say it," she again ordered with all the pity of an axe murderer.

None.

Mitchell knew what she wanted. Dreaded it, in fact. Never, ever would he say it. She could kill him first. He sealed his lips tight and glared at her defiantly.

Annoyance made her freckled button nose wrinkle. "Stop being so freakn' stubborn. You know we're meant to be together, so just admit it." Such certainty from a ten-year-old girl who still played with dolls.

Looking into her familiar countenance surround by bobbing red pigtails, a well-known visage he'd encountered almost daily since she was a baby, he screwed up his face. "Eew, Francine. That's just gross. You're like a sister to me."

His announcement, as expected, didn't go over well. Her face tightened in irritation. "I am not your freakn' sister," she yelled as she sat up and placed her hands on her waist, the picture of thwarted indignation.

"Close enough," he growled, suddenly rolling his body sideways, jolting her off of him. Free, he sprang to his feet and ran, fast as he could, but he still heard her holler.

"You might escape for now, Mitchell, but you can't run forever. One day, you, you'll come to your senses and admit you're my mate."

Like freakn' hell.

Chapter One

Years later…

Figured her car would decide to die without warning, probably because the warranty on it ran out the week before.

"Stupid piece of crap." Francine slapped the steering wheel and got out of her car. She glared at the offending piece of junk, wondering just how she would now make it to her best friend's baby shower in time. Sure, she could have stripped and turned furry, running the rest of the way, but then how would she carry the damned present she'd bought for the occasion? Arriving empty handed seemed so gauche no matter the reason. And, given the awkward size of the gift, she couldn't exactly carry it in her canine mouth.

Sighing, she yanked out her cell phone, only to curse at the black screen. She'd forgotten to charge it—again.

"Great, just freakn' great. Now what the hell am I supposed to do?" Hands on her hips, she peered up and down the road, still at least three miles from where she needed to go. Just her luck, she didn't spot hide nor hair of anything, not on this secluded stretch of road, part of the reason the little neighborhood at its end proved so popular with shifter families.

What to do? It occurred to her that other guests were expected, so perhaps if she started walking, one would happen to come along and give her a lift. Never mind the fact she ran late and was probably the last guest to arrive. Surely fate wouldn't let her miss her BFF's big moment?

Grabbing the present with its big yellow bow, Francine began walking in heels meant to look pretty and elongate her short legs. They lasted five minutes. The third time she stumbled in the gravel, she ripped them off her feet and threw them in the woods. Five minutes after that, she regretted her haste as the rough pavement underfoot didn't exactly scream comfort.

Fifteen minutes into her walk, hot, annoyed, and her feet dirty, she plopped herself on top her present in the middle of the road, determined to wait for a vehicle even if it took all day. The box, of course, dented under her weight and she jumped off it with another curse. *Great, just great. Could this day get any more annoying?*

The attempt to straighten out the box ended up with it looking even more lopsided and she restrained an urge to kick it. Thankfully, luck finally came her way before she gave in to an urge to go psychotic on the gift. A rumble in the distance had her peering up the road. Waiting for fate to drop the other shoe, she didn't move as the sound approached. But it didn't start to rain, and the vehicle didn't do a sudden u-turn to head in the other direction. She perked up when she noted the motorcycle coasting to a stop in front of her, then sighed. While guys who rode bikes were hot in her book, and any other time she would have jumped on the chance for a ride, unfortunately, given the mangled present she still needed to bring, he just wouldn't do.

Clad in leather, the rider wore a shorty helmet along with a pair of aviator sunglasses that reflected her own image back. A bandanna covered his lower mouth and jaw, a protection against eating stray bugs that effectively rendered him featureless.

He cocked his head at her. "Need a ride?" he shouted, his mirth at her situation evident even over the engine noise.

She took a second to admire the size of him; tall, wide, and sexy in his riding gear. But, she was already spoken for. Kind of. Mitchell would eventually come to his senses and realize they were meant for each other. Hopefully before all the eggs in her ovaries expired.

"Thanks, but I don't want to leave the present behind. I'm going to a baby shower."

"What a coincidence, so am I. The present's not a problem. I've got great balance. I'll hold it if you hold onto me."

Another guest for Naomi's party, which meant he was a shifter, just like her. The smell of exhaust made her unable to sniff what species he belonged to. Not that it mattered—she already had a man, sort of, once he stopped acting like a stubborn ass.

Unsure of how her rescuer would manage to drive and hold onto the gift at the same time, she hesitated, however, not spotting any other signs of life, she didn't really have a choice. It seemed like his offer was the only way she'd get to the party fashionably late.

"Fine, I accept. But if you drop it, I'll have to hurt you," she warned.

"Promise?" This time, she definitely couldn't mistake the humor.

"Pig." She didn't say it with heat, though, and he laughed, a rumbly sound that tickled over her and made her inner wolf wake with a start to peer with interest at the stranger.

Strolling over to his bike while holding the gift, she let him take the package from her then eyed the small wedge of seat behind him.

"Are you sure I'll fit?" She owned panties with more crotch room than that thing.

"Just hold on tight, baby, and I'll do the rest."

His words sent a blush to her cheeks, especially since he said them in a sultry tone that rendered his meaning quite clear. She just wished she could see his face to see if he joked or not. At five-foot-two and packing some curves, she wasn't the type to have guys hit on her out of the blue, not until they'd had a few beers anyways.

Actually, on second thought, better I don't see his face. He's probably butt ugly, and besides, I'm almost taken.

Bracing one hand on his shoulder, she managed to swing one leg over to plop herself on the sliver of seat, wedging it between her thighs. Its pressing hardness along with the vibrating thrum of the engine between her legs made for some interesting sensations.

The driver's free hand grasped hers and pulled it around his torso, tugging her into his body. "Hold me tight, baby, and I'll take us where we need to go."

Screw the shower, going to heaven came to mind as her body reacted to his proximity. Wrapping her arms around him, she fought an urge to let her hands stroke up and down his chest. Even clad in leather, she could tell he owned a hard, muscled physique. Words, for once, failed her, which would have cracked her BFF up. But what shocked Francine most was her wolf's reaction. Her inner canine wanted to sniff the stranger up and down and follow it up with a lick. Usually that type of reaction only happened when she thought of Mitchell.

"Ready?" he prompted.

Nodding, she held on for dear life as he gunned the bike and they shot off, his one arm held out holding the gift while the other did the rest. It occurred to Francine to wonder how he intended to drive one handed, but he seemed to be managing it fine, so she decided to keep her mouth shut lest she distract him. Besides, she preferred to concentrate on how she felt plastered against him. A small part of her winced that she cheated of a sort on Mitchell, the man who wouldn't claim her even though she knew he was her fated mate. But another part of her, the same part that made her give Tommy Keller her virginity at her grade twelve prom out of spite, wanted her to squeeze closer and drop her hands to see if his thighs felt as muscled as they looked.

I'm such a skank, she thought. A horny one, who after the Tommy incident, vowed to stay away from men until Mitchell came to his senses, a vow she broke within a month when she heard about his

12

newest girlfriend. Jealous—and pissed he kept fighting fate—she went to a bar to get drunk and bang some guy whose name she usually couldn't recall the next day.

However her days of sleeping around to quell her irritation and heartache were things of the past now. She'd turned over a new leaf. As of nine months ago, she no longer did that. No sirree, once she saw Naomi, the biggest bitch she knew—God, she loved that girl—find her mates—the skank lucked out and got two—she just knew her time was about to come. She didn't want the scent of another man clinging to her when it did. Although, she wouldn't have minded seeing a jealous Mitchell. Actually, just seeing Mitchell, who'd avoided her like she suffered from the plague since they were kids, would have proven an improvement. Currently, the only thing she ever saw of Mitchell was his ass as it went flying out the door to escape her. The chicken.

It hadn't always been that way. He'd tolerated her well enough as his kid sister's best friend, but that all changed when they got to their teens. She'd kept waiting for him to make his move. He didn't, so she had, sometimes with a little too much enthusiasm and force. He rebuffed her, over and over. She'd grown to hate his oft repeated, "But I think of you as a sister." Jerk, like his sister ever tried to give him tongue.

So, despite how wet Mr. Hot-In-Leather made her, she wouldn't do anything about it, because she just knew if Mitchell would let himself stay in a room with her for longer than thirty seconds, he'd finally realize she'd grown up. And then he'd claim her so they could live happily ever after, before she went postal and killed his furry ass.

* * * *

Mitchell kept peering out the bay window. He thought he'd managed to do so unobtrusively until the cuff that caught him upside of the head.

Turning, he glared at his very pregnant baby sister who smirked at him. "Aww, aren't you so cute acting all eager-beaver like. Don't worry, big brother. Francine will be here soon."

"What makes you think I'm watching for her?" It annoyed him that his sister knew whom he searched for, but for the wrong reason. Yes, he kept an eye out for Francine, but only because he needed a head-start to escape.

"Oh, please. You do this every time you know she's coming over. Hell, the last time, you almost took Mom out in your hurry to dive out the back door. Talk about pathetic. Just give in already. The whole family knows you two are meant for each other. So stop acting like such a pussy. Why not act like the dog you are and claim her?"

"That's rich coming from, Mrs. I-wanna-marry-a-human," he mocked in a high-pitched voice. That earned him a scowl and a whack in the arm.

"And look what happened to me. Bitch slapped with two men instead of one."

14

"Wait, do you think if I keep holding out, then fate will give me two or three women?" He leered, and then ducked as she swung again. Chuckling, he quite enjoyed his sister's annoyed red face.

All too soon, her face smoothed into a calm mask, one he knew better than to trust. "From what I hear, Francine is worth two women in bed. Betcha she'd have you begging for mercy and walking funny if you gave her a chance."

Mitchell spoke through gritted teeth. "Would you stop saying shit like that? Francine is like a sister to me. The idea of doing anything with her is just gross."

"Blah, blah, blah. You know, I believed that whole sister line you fed us ten years ago when you guys were still kids, but seriously, Mitchell. You haven't seen or talked to her in at least the last five or six years. She's changed, so how can you still claim that?"

"Because." What no one else seemed to recognize, except him, was while he'd always found Francine cute, she didn't make him want to throw her down and ravish her. If they truly were mates, why hadn't the mating fever hit him? The wild urge to claim her, growing in intensity until he couldn't help himself and he fucked her until they both passed out from pleasure. He'd heard enough stories to know that in a true mating, hormones went wild, and while his heart did race when he knew Francine got close, and his palms sweated, it appeared more a recurrence of his childhood fear that she would tackle him and force him into something he didn't want—like a sloppy kiss tasting of watermelon gum. He didn't want that for either of them, not when it meant the right person, their true mate, still hadn't come along.

"Idiot." His sister cuffed him again before she waddled off, a prime example of a mating done right. Ornery and scary as shit, his baby sister found happiness in the arms of not one, but two shifters. Ethan and Javier, a bear and jaguar, who'd managed to tone down some of Naomi's wilder impulses, but more remarkably, loved her for her feisty nature. Sick bastards.

The rumble of a motor drew his attention back to the window and he wondered if the time for his departure had arrived, but no, he didn't spot Francine's blue Hyundai Accent. Instead, a sleek motorcycle pulled up out front. Then Mitchell blinked because if he weren't mistaken, the driver held a present out to the side in one hand as he coasted to a stop. Only once he lowered his arm, did Mitchell notice his passenger. His heart sped up and his jaw dropped as Francine unhooked her arms from around the guy's waist and slid off the bike.

Of course, this Francine looked vastly different from the high school one he recalled with pigtails and braces, although she remained just as short. But the rest of her, shit, when had her plumpness turned into curves that gave her an hourglass shape? Since when did she have breasts that strained her blouse, and wild red hair that corkscrewed around her face and brought attention to her full-lipped smile? He'd spent so much time avoiding her, he'd not actually ever seen the grown up version. Not that it changed anything.

The driver slid off the bike, and set the present down before he yanked down the bandanna covering the lower half of his face. He then pulled off his helmet, shaking out shaggy black hair, and even from where he stood shielded by the sheer curtains, Mitchell couldn't miss the masculine grin he threw Francine. It roused his wolf, who growled with hackles raised. Mitchell didn't bother to stop and try to figure out what about this guy put his beast on edge –or why—suddenly angry, he just stormed out to confront them.

Stomping down the porch steps, Francine turned his way, delight lighting her expression as she saw him. And damn it all if he didn't feel an answering tug—in his cock. Totally inappropriate. To ignore her and his reaction, he looked at her companion. The strange dude, who'd pulled off his aviator glasses and tucked them in his pocket, flicked him a disinterested glance before letting his gaze stray downwards to ogle Francine's jean-clad ass. It made Mitchell, both the man and his beast, growl in annoyance.

Coming to a stop before a little girl who'd grown into a much too pretty woman, Mitchell's terse words wiped the smile off Francine's face. "And just what the hell do you think you were doing, young lady, riding a motorcycle without a helmet?"

Ire flashed in her eyes, and she planted her fists on rounded hips before retorting. "Whatever happened to 'Hi, Francine?' or "How's it going, Francine?' I don't see you in, what, five years, and you freak out because I rode a few miles on a bike without a helmet? I'm a shapeshifter. Short of decapitation, I'll heal."

"A few miles?" he shouted back. "It's at least thirty clicks from here to your place. Your hotshot boyfriend is lucky the cops didn't pull you over."

"He's not my boyfriend," she growled. "Although, if he were, what we did together would be none of your business."

"And might I add, we'd do some very *interesting* things." The tanned biker, who this close, Mitchell recognized by scent as some sort of large cat, should have kept his mouth shut. Mitchell's fist came flying out of nowhere to hit him in the jaw. Not that it rocked the bastard. The big guy took it and grinned wider.

"Is that the best you can do, wolfie? I've had human girls give me love taps harder than that."

A red haze descended over him at that point, and Mitchell couldn't stop himself from snarling and slamming into the other man, sending them to the ground in a tussling heap, one his wolf entirely approved of.

Damned cat. I'll teach him to sniff around a guy's adopted little sister.

Chapter Two

Francine couldn't stop herself from gaping at the wrestling men. She still couldn't quite grasp what happened. *If I didn't know better, I'd say Mitchell was jealous.* Crazy, of course. He'd made it perfectly clear he didn't think of her that way.

What didn't surprise her was the way he'd yelled at her just like he would with his sister Naomi. A part of her wished she could dislike him. After all, look at the way he'd just treated her, and in front of the gorgeous looking stranger who'd rescued her. Heck, his reluctance to even be in the same room as her should have made kicking him to the curb a cinch. But, she couldn't stop her heart from beating faster, and her cleft from moistening as she watched the two big men trading blows. If only they would get naked as they fought. Talk about real entertainment.

"Not even here two minutes and already causing trouble, I see," her friend announced, coming down the steps, her belly leading the way. Behind Naomi strode Javier, his step light as he bounded over the rolling combatants, followed by Ethan, a giant of a man who could recite poetry one evening, and crush a whole team of lacrosse players the next. Naomi was such a lucky bitch.

Pursing her lips, Francine glared at the snarling men. "It was Mitchell who started it. I was just trying to say thanks to the guy who rescued me from the road after my car broke down when Mitchell got all bossy and then attacked him."

"Hmmm." Naomi peered at her brother pensively for a moment. "Interesting. I wonder what set him off?"

"He's your brother. Since when does anybody in your family need a reason to fight?" Francine said dryly. She'd often joked they should hand helmets out at the door.

Naomi laughed. "True. But they're usually better behaved when they come over. You know how Ethan gets when they upset me."

Francine snorted. Naomi kept insisting she was a delicate freakn' flower—Not!—and both her mates treated her like one. Ethan usually acted as the peacemaker—his huge fist acting as a deterrent to misbehavior—while Javier used his smooth tongue to ensure nothing disturbed her, not even her family. Again, luckiest skank alive.

"So who is the hottie anyway?" Francine asked, wincing as Mitchell bashed the biker's head onto the ground. She then bit her lip as the tanned stranger head butted him back.

"That would be my baby brother, Alejandro," Javier said with a shake of his head as he slid his arm around Naomi's rounded middle. "And, as usual, he's causing shit wherever he goes."

"It wasn't his fault," Francine said in his defense. "Mitchell swung first."

Javier chuckled. "They always swing first when Alejandro's around, usually because he's done or said something he shouldn't."

Remembering his innuendo, Francine couldn't deny it. Even funnier, though, she'd enjoyed it.

The combatants rolled off the walkway, still trying to get the upper hand, onto the lawn. Their brawl brought them precariously close to a well-ordered cluster of blooms, hand planted by Naomi.

"Ethan, they're going to crush my pretty flowers," Naomi barked, more concerned about her garden than her brother's now bleeding nose.

With a quirk of his lips, Naomi's big teddy bear bent over, grabbed the fighters by the arm and yanked them apart. "Enough, or I'll beat you both," he rumbled.

Few people were stupid enough to mess with a Kodiak bear, and these two, despite their heated blood, were no exception. Mitchell stumbled to his feet with a glower while Alejandro lay there with a grin and messy hair that made him even sexier. "But we were just getting to know each other."

Mitchell growled. His fists, clenched at his side, turned almost white in direct contrast to his bright red, extremely annoyed expression.

"Stop pissing off Naomi's brother or I'll let Ethan have a go at you," Javier warned.

"I could use the exercise," added the bear with a vicious smile that made more than one lacrosse player on the floor run the other way.

Alejandro laughed before springing to his feet. Ignoring a still bristling Mitchell, he headed to Naomi, enveloping her in a gentle hug.

"Naomi, my sweet sister-in-law, you look more gorgeous each time I see you. If you weren't already taken…"

"Yes, I know, we'd fuck like wild animals until the next cutie caught your eye."

"Ah, but we'd have so much fun until that happened," he said with a wink.

While Francine found their byplay entertaining, her wolf, for some reason, didn't, and growled in her head.

Thankfully, she didn't have to listen to her bitch's weird pms-ing for long as Javier yanked Alejandro from Naomi's arms. Javier squeezed him in a hug and said in a low tone, not low enough for shifter ears to miss, "Grab her ass again, and I'll cut off your hand."

"Brother, you wound me," Alejandro replied, hugging his older sibling back before escaping.

"Not as much as I will," Ethan announced in a cheerful voice. Alejandro blanched a bit, but shook the bear's hand, grunting when Ethan snagged him in a bear hug.

When he released him, Alejandro looked red in the face as his chest heaved for air.

Naomi laughed. "Javier, you and your brothers almost make my family look normal."

"God forbid," her mate replied, rolling his eyes. "I guess I should introduce everyone starting with the little trouble maker here. This is Alejandro, my youngest and most annoying brother." Facing his brother he said, "The guy who is trying to kill you with his gaze is

Naomi's brother, Mitchell. And the redhead you somehow kidnapped on your way in is Naomi's best friend, which means off limits, Francine."

Francine could only sputter. "Javier!"

"What? I'm just making things clear now because I'd hate to have to kick his ass later."

"Such a good husband," Naomi purred, patting his arm. "He knows which side of his bread to butter."

Francine could only roll her eyes as her best friend and her mate gazed at each other sappily. When they exchanged a smooch, she put a finger in her mouth and pretended to gag, which made Alejandro chuckle while Mitchell just frowned. Spoilsport.

"Francine, is that the name of the vision of loveliness I found languishing on the road?" Alejandro threw himself on a knee in front of Francine who blushed as he continued to wax poetic. "It was such an honor and a pleasure for me to be able to aide you in continuing your journey. Might I say, you can ride with me anytime?" He waggled his brows and gave her a suggestive grin that caused her to blush, giggle—and wet herself in a naughty spot all at once.

"A pleasure," she murmured, letting him grab her hand and kiss it. The tip of his tongue on her skin along with his lips made her breath catch, and butterflies spontaneously came to life in her tummy. She snatched her hand back, her cheeks heating at the reaction of her body, a reaction that didn't go unnoticed.

Snorting, Mitchell stalked off, muttering, "You've got to be freakn' kidding me. Who the fuck falls for that shit?"

Watching him go, Francine couldn't stop her sigh of disappointment.

"What is it, baby? Don't tell me you're sorry to see that stick in the mud go?"

"That uptight stick is my mate, or will be once he lets himself unbend enough to see it," she retorted.

With an incredulous look, Alejandro looked at Mitchell's retreating form then back at her. "He's an idiot if he can't see what a prize you are."

"The idiot gene runs in the family. I should know," snorted Naomi. "Now, can we go inside? My back is killing me and I want to open presents."

Francine lingered for a moment, watching the direction Mitchell disappeared in, wondering what it would take to make him claim her. Did his wolf not get agitated whenever they met? Of course, they'd not seen each other in years, through no fault of her own. That man knew how to freakn' run and hide. But still, seeing him again, all delicious six-foot-three inches of him, her bitch went haywire, her heart sped up, and a tingle swept through her body.

Which, oddly enough, also happened when I met Alejandro. Could she have mistaken the mating urge all these years with pure and simple lust? But no, she'd known desire before, and it didn't make her want to throw her self-respect to the wind and chase after him so she could tackle his lanky frame and tear off his clothes.

She would have pondered it some more, but she found herself grabbed and thrown over a shoulder, a wide one.

"Um, Ethan, wrong woman."

"Naomi said to carry your mooning ass inside."

"I'm sure she didn't mean that literally."

"She's pregnant and extremely hormonal. I'm not taking chances."

"I heard that!" Naomi hollered.

"See," Ethan whispered.

A giggle escaped Francine. Some people might have called her nuts for wanting to belong to this family, but personally, she couldn't imagine anything more awesome, even if most family dinners required a person to wear a helmet and padding for protection. Still, despite the violent tendencies, the love they all had for each other more than made up for it.

* * * *

Alejandro hit the bathroom first to wash the dust and blood off his face before he grabbed a beer. He needed the bitter brew to help him assimilate what had just happened. Chugging it, though, didn't give him enough time to wonder why the little redhead he'd picked up on his way here made his cat purr. Or why he'd wanted to beat the hell out of that upstart wolf—and still did. It especially didn't answer why he wanted to commit suicide by launching himself at Ethan, who carried the little firecracker inside.

Thankfully, he stayed alive, managing to curb his impulse to attack the giant Kodiak when he set Francine down. However, it did nothing to curb the interest of his cat, who prowled in his mind, suggesting he get closer to her for a sniff.

But despite her allure, he needed to stay away. After all, he was simply a guest here for a short time while the troubles back home calmed. Entertaining himself with her, while fun, probably wasn't worth the hassle because the lady in question was spoken for, kind of. Not that he cared what that arrogant idiot Mitchell thought. It was his sister-in-law, Naomi, that scared him. If he hurt her best friend, chances were he'd end up missing a body part or two.

However, deciding to give Francine a wide berth and doing so proved two completely different things. As if he owned no control over his own body, he found himself immediately going to stand behind her when she sank onto Naomi's couch beside an older woman. She ignored him, and miffed at the unusualness of it, he did the same back, perusing the crowd in the room.

Alejandro didn't know most of the people, having only visited once before on a stopover. He'd gotten to know Naomi when Javier brought her home to show off to his family. The visit ended up vastly entertaining as Javier—his older, lusty brother—showed a possessive streak none of them had encountered before. It made their flirting with his mate so much fun, until Naomi put a stop to it, her grip on Miguel's balls leaving him squeaking for days as she explained that while she found it funny how they taunted Javier, if they touched her again, she'd rip them off. Somehow, they didn't doubt her ability to do so.

What a woman, even if she's not my type. He preferred not to worry about getting hurt when he slept with a woman. His gaze dropped to the top of Francine's head. He couldn't see the little firecracker hurting a fly.

Sliding into the vacated spot beside Francine, he couldn't stop the jolt of awareness that made his body flare to life as his thigh brushed hers. A sharp inhalation of her breath told him she felt it too. She turned startled eyes his way and he grinned, enjoying the blush that crept into her freckled cheeks.

While not gorgeous by model standards, he couldn't deny her girl next door appeal. Wild-haired, bright-eyed, and with lips that could only improve if they wrapped around his cock, she owned a set of curves begging for a man's touch. What an idiot that Mitchell was for not claiming her. *I could bite her and steal her out from under him, then the little wolf would belong to me.* He almost recoiled from her when his thoughts veered into that unknown territory. Alejandro did not claim women. Flirt with them, fuck them, and make them cry as he left, yes, but mark one to keep as his own? Why bind himself to one when he could enjoy a variety?

It occurred to him that the challenge she posed with her I'm-taken-but-not stance probably made her appealing. Anything else was

27

just foolish, or caused by a lack of sleep. He'd needed to put as many miles as possible between him and a certain situation he'd fled.

"Are you going to stare at me all night, or are you mentally conversing with aliens?" she asked, breaking his inner train of thought.

He recovered quickly. "Just wondering how that overgrown dog hasn't recognized what a gem you are?"

Again, that beautiful blush colored her cheeks. "Mitchell has issues with seeing me as something other than a sister. Naomi and I have been hanging out since we were babies. Apparently, that makes getting with me gross."

"I'd say he's a moron if he hasn't noticed you've grown up, and might I say, nicely." He flashed her the hundred watt grin that dropped panties wherever he went.

Hers stayed intact. A snort escaped her. "My God, are you always like this?"

"Like what? Charming and handsome?"

"Conceited and flirty."

"Now you wound me," he said, clasping her hand and pressing it to his chest. Again, a jolt went through him and his heart rate increased.

"I doubt it," she replied, but her eyes remained locked to his and she didn't pull away.

"Alejandro, stop flirting with my brother's almost mate and come over here to meet my family." With regret, he let go of her hand, and she ducked her head as he stood. *Thank God my leather pants are tight,* he thought as he made sure his untucked t-shirt hung over his groin, further hiding his semi-erection.

I really need to get laid if a simple conversation at a baby shower is making me horny. He usually enjoyed better self-control.

Linking her arm in his, Naomi dragged him around, introducing him to folks scattered around the room. He shook hands with several of her brothers, none of whom gave him an urge to punch their lights out like the annoying Mitchell. He met her uncomfortable-looking father, Geoffrey, and several aunts and cousins. He fawned over Naomi's mother's hand, which made the older woman laugh and her husband glare. By the time they'd come full circle, his head spun with names and faces, the place packed with shifters. Judging by the tic on Ethan's face, he recognized the possibility of an explosion with so many animals in one place. And everyone knew how Naomi disliked chaos in her house.

This could get interesting, but not as interesting as the round ass he caught a glimpse of, bent over and straining the fabric covering it, as Francine began to hand Naomi the gifts.

Maybe he'd acted a little hastily in deciding to not pursue the little firecracker. Perhaps she wouldn't find herself averse to a little strings-free fun. He'd just have to make sure Naomi and her mates didn't find out. Sneaky sex in other words. God, that made the prospect even more exciting. But how to get her alone?

He trusted fate, and his usual luck with women, would see him getting to know the feisty redhead better, make that naked and sweaty.

* * * *

Annoyed, but unable to figure out the exact cause, Mitchell stalked home and flopped full length on his parents' couch, trying not to feel like such a coward for fleeing. For years it had become second nature to avoid Francine, but tonight, actually seeing her, smelling her for the first time since their teen years, he discovered something he'd never expected. *She's hot!* Actually, more than hot; sexy, curvy and with an enticing aroma that made him want to sink to his knees and bay at her like he'd worship the moon.

It seemed almost sick to think it. Little pig-tailed Francine, pain in his ass, with her shrill voice, raucous ways, and determined chasing, had gone from annoying pest to luscious beauty. Even closing his eyes, he couldn't erase the sight of her from his mind, but in his mental vision, she wore nothing, just some freckles begging that he count them with his lips.

Cock hardening, he jumped up from the couch and paced. *Wrong, so wrong.* A temporary aberration because he'd not shagged anyone in a while. He'd rectify that problem ASAP because no matter what his prick thought, Francine was off limits. And as for his wolf's interest, it stemmed probably from a desire to protect her from that suave Casanova sniffing around her. Of course, some might have seen his outburst as jealousy, but Mitchell knew better. He'd have done the same thing for Naomi. *But Francine is a grown woman,* his mind slyly reminded. *She can date whoever she wants.* Mitchell growled and his fist lashed out to connect with the tough wood paneling installed years ago at their mother's behest because she'd tired of the holes in the plaster.

Obviously needing to vent, he headed to the basement gym and the sorry-looking punching bag, duct taped because of the abuse suffered over the years. It was while he pummeled the inanimate object into submission that he realized something. If Francine's car was broken down, how would she get home?

Whacking at the heavy bag, he tried to convince himself that Naomi would get one of her mates or cousins to take Francine back. But the more he tried to tell himself that, the more he couldn't help picturing Javier's brother with Francine's arms wrapped around him as they took off on that death trap of his. Not on his watch, they wouldn't.

Quickly, he showered, dressed, then drove down the road and parked, waiting for Francine to emerge, too chicken to go inside where he just knew the whole family, namely his mother and Naomi, would watch him with arched brows. He told himself as he sat waiting that he did this for her own safety. He wouldn't want his sister riding with a stranger at night with no helmet.

But even as he kept saying that to himself, he couldn't help hearing maniacal laughter and a mocking chant in his head. *Liar, liar, pants on fire.* What a shame he couldn't punch himself. Aw well, maybe if he got lucky, he'd get the chance to punch someone else.

31

Chapter Three

As the baby shower wound down, Francine began to wonder how she'd get home. A taxi from here would cost more cash than she carried. Her car at least had been towed. Aunt Kerry, upon hearing her troubles, called her husband, a mechanic, to tow it to his garage.

Approaching her friend, surrounded by miniature pieces of clothing and baby toys, Francine couldn't help smiling at her obvious happiness.

"Francine, did you see these?" Naomi exclaimed, holding up a pair of tiny running shoes. "Too freakn' cute."

"Disgustingly so," she giggled. "God, I can't believe you're about to pop twins."

"Good thing I've got two daddies to help handle them," Naomi added.

"And two awesome boobies," Javier said with a laugh, leaning over the back of her chair to honk them.

"Pig!" Naomi yelled, slapping at his hand. "We have guests."

"We have Francine and my brother left. Everyone else scattered before you handed them a mop and broom to clean."

"I'm not that anal," she muttered.

"Of course you're not," Francine said, patting her hand with a snicker.

"Bitch."

"Skank."

"Love you, Francine."

"Love you too, Naomi."

"Can I love you both?" asked Alejandro, only to choke as Ethan came up behind him and grabbed him in a headlock.

Javier moved around the chair to sit on the armrest, draping his arm over the back of his mate's shoulders. "Are you sure I can't kill him and turn him into a rug for the nursery?"

"No, you may not. Do you know how hard it is to get blood out of hardwood floors? And don't forget, I speak from experience. Besides, I need him to drive Francine home."

Automatically, her mouth opened to protest. "Oh no, I couldn't. I'll just take a cab, if you loan me a few dollars."

"Nonsense, my brother will take you. And he will behave," Javier added with a glare in Alejandro's direction.

"But—"

"No buts. He doesn't mind, do you, little brother?"

Released by Ethan, Alejandro grinned as he rubbed his neck. "My pleasure." He winked and Javier groaned, but Francine's reaction followed the pattern it had all day. She warmed and blushed. She, who could fake a screaming orgasm in public, who could skinny dip naked in the daytime, who could walk up to a good-looking guy in a bar and say, 'Wanna fuck?' But apparently, when the good-looking Alejandro opened his mouth or touched her, she turned into some freakn' virgin. Worse, she couldn't stop her bitch from yipping in excitement every time he got near. Weird, because her inner wolf did the same thing around Mitchell. What could it mean? Sure, her BFF had two mates, but given her temper, she needed them. Francine on the other hand, tended toward an even humor, and while frisky in the bedroom, just needed one man, AKA Mitchell, to keep her happy. But someone needed to explain that to her wolf, apparently.

"Earth to Francine, are you coming or what?"

She wished. Again, that blush rode her cheeks as she stood and they all trooped out front so she could leave with Alejandro.

Naomi hugged her tight. "Sorry about what happened with Mitchell."

"Not your fault your brother acted like a douche bag. Go and put your feet up. Don't want those babies popping out too early."

After squeezing hugs by Naomi's mates, she turned and walked down the driveway to where Alejandro waited, looking entirely too gorgeous. She'd no sooner reached him than a familiar form got out of a parked car and stalked toward them.

Surprise made her jaw drop. "Mitchell? What are you doing here?"

"I've come to give you a ride home."

"She's already got one," Alejandro said, handing her his helmet.

The man she'd loved forever turned to snarl at Alejandro. "She's not riding with you, cat."

"She doesn't belong to you, so what makes you think it's your decision?"

"Because I said so."

Oh, seriously, Mitchell hadn't just said that. Francine didn't say anything yet, letting her annoyance grow as she crossed her arms and watched them argue over her. Irritating as she found it, she couldn't deny it was also kind of hot.

Alejandro snorted. "Aren't you just the little dictator? Tell you what, why don't we let the lady decide?"

Two pairs of eyes veered to look at her, and Francine had an irrational urge to stomp her foot. How often did she get two men fighting over her? And why did one of them have to be Mitchell, who acted like an ass earlier? Going with him meant rewarding him for bad behavior, and yet refusing meant missing a chance for him to realize that she'd grown up. What to do?

Taking a deep breath, she said. "Thanks, Mitchell, but I wouldn't want to put you out. Besides, Alejandro needs a place to stay for the night and I've offered him my couch."

Okay, so she fibbed a little. She waited to see if Alejandro would call her on it, but other than a slight widening of his eyes, he covered for her. "Yes, thankfully, Francine has agreed to save me from hearing the raucous noise of my brother making love to his mate."

"No." Mitchell said only the one word. Nothing more, but he did cross his arms.

The situation got more and more interesting because now Francine couldn't deny he sounded like a jealous boyfriend. *Or an overprotective brother.* For the sake of her vanity, she'd pretend it was the former. "I'm sorry, but that's not your decision to make," she replied haughtily. "See you around."

She waved at him before shoving the helmet onto her head. The scent of man, musky and enticing, surrounded her, and she couldn't help the tingle that went through her. To hide it, she stepped around Mitchell and clambered onto the back of the bike. She wrapped her arms around the already seated Alejandro, and pretended to not notice Mitchell's glower.

"Hold on tight, baby." With a rumble of power that vibrated between her legs, they took off. She couldn't deny the rush of excitement as Alejandro drove, her occasional prompting guiding them to her townhouse. Parking in her driveway, she pulled the helmet off with a laugh and a shake of her head that send her curls bouncing.

"That was fun!"

"More fun than making Mitchell crazed with jealousy?" he asked with a smirk.

"Ha. I wish. I'm sure he's already convinced himself he was doing it to protect my honor. Jerk." She dug her keys out of her pocket and led him to her front door. Unlocking it, she swung it open, hyper aware that Alejandro stood behind her. A part of her wondered if inviting him over was still such a good idea, especially given how her whole body—and wolf—reacted around him.

"Well, I guess I'll be on my way now."

Francine, half in the door, turned to give him a puzzled look. "Why? You and I both know that you won't sleep a wink if Naomi goes at it with your brother and Ethan. Trust me, been there, done that, and it is beyond loud. And paying for a hotel is dumb when I've got a perfectly good couch." She owned an even more comfortable bed. *Bad, bad girl.*

Uncertainty crossed his face. "I probably shouldn't. Javier will kill me if he thinks I've dared touch his mate's best friend."

"Were you planning to?" she asked saucily, feeling more in control now that he seemed unsure.

"I shouldn't, but you are quite the tempting dish."

"Flattery will get you everywhere," she laughed. "Just not in my pants." Because despite his allure, and he owned plenty, she strived to make Mitchell jealous, not drive a wedge between them, not when he'd finally taken note of her. "Now get your ass inside, and let's have a beer to celebrate."

He followed her inside asking, "Celebrating what?"

"The fact that there was only one fist fight at the party and it was outside. That's got to be a record for Naomi's family."

Javier snorted as he followed her to the kitchen and parked himself on a stool. "If you think her family is bad, then you should meet mine. Although, usually, it's not so much the family fighting as it is angry fathers and scorned lovers. We tend to leave a trail of broken hearts."

"Gee, a great line like that and yet you still manage to get laid."

He grinned at her. "It's my great big…" He paused and winked. "Smile."

Francine laughed. "Oh, you're a bad one. No wonder the girls drop their panties for you." The phone rang and she leaned over to grab it. "House of pleasure, how may I orally please you?" she purred, recognizing the number.

"You are such a nasty skank," Naomi exclaimed. "I see you made it home safe. But, I've got to say, I'm surprised at your choice in rides."

"Just because Mitchell suddenly decided to notice I exist doesn't give him the right to act like a jerk. Besides, you should have seen the look on his face when I turned him down. Freakn' priceless."

Laughter pealed from the ear piece and Francine held it away with a cringe that made Alejandro grin before he sipped at his beer.

"So, when should I expect Javier's furball of a brother home?"

"Tomorrow."

"What? Francine, don't tell me you're going to sleep with him?"

She rolled her eyes. "Of course not. But, I figured he'd enjoy my quiet couch more than your noisy spare room."

"My guest room isn't… Oh, you are such a bitch. Like you're so freakn' quiet."

"I know I'm not." Francine began to moan into the microphone to Naomi's laughter and Alejandro's widening gaze. She got to the part where she panted and screamed, "Yes! Yes!" before letting it taper off as Naomi giggled hysterically on the other end. Poor Alejandro just stared at her with a glazed expression. She winked at him. "Talk to you later, my oversized BFF. Oh, and don't pop out those babies having too much fun."

Naomi blew her a raspberry before hanging up. Francine took a sip of her beer, eyeing Alejandro's gaping mouth. "What?"

"I can't believe you just did that."

"You mean the fake orgasm?" She beamed. "I know. I'm good. I should have been a phone sex operator or something, but instead, I work as a legal secretary. How boring, huh?"

"So, what does a real orgasm sound like?"

"Wouldn't you like to know?" She winked, horny, but at the same time, at ease. Unusual, given she drove most men nuts when she spoke and they did anything to shut her up.

"Actually, I would, but that would be wrong. Right?" He didn't sound certain.

Funny, neither was she, but she agreed anyway. "So very wrong. Mitchell's my one and only. Stupid jerk who won't come to his senses."

"Are you sure he's the one?"

"I've known he was my mate since I learned to crawl," she retorted. "I didn't understand what I felt, though, until I talked to my grandma about the whole mating thing. Once I knew, I tried for years to get him to admit he felt it too, but that man is slippery like a wet eel."

A puzzled look crossed his face. "And yet, you still want him?"

A depressed sigh made her deflate. "I know, super dumb huh? He keeps rejecting me and I keep going back for more. But the heart wants what it wants, or in this case, my wolf wants. Figures I'd be fated to mate with the one man who needs me to tie him down and beat him until he finally stops hiding from the truth."

"Mmm, stop your dirty talk about bondage or I might forget I'm a gentleman," he said with a leer and a chuckle.

She grinned. "You are really good for the ego, you know? I might just have to keep you around." *Naked and tied to my bed.* The mental image made her squirm in her seat.

"And people say I'm a flirt."

Blowing him a kiss, she cocked her head and studied him as she sipped on her beer. Gorgeous didn't come close to describing Alejandro with his tanned skin, dark chocolate eyes, and sensual lips. He would be so easy to fall for. "So what about you? What are you running from?"

"Who, me?" His wide-eyed false innocence made her laugh.

"Get caught in the wrong bed?" she guessed.

"That happens more often than you'd think. All I try to do is bring a little pleasure into a woman's life and yet do their husbands or boyfriends understand?"

Holding in her snicker proved impossible and they both broke into gales of laughter. "You are so bad," she gasped.

"Or good, it depends on your definition. You should use that to your advantage."

"I don't understand."

"Your Mitchell situation. Maybe your reluctant wolf just needs the right incentive."

"Meaning?"

"Well, you say he finally noticed you for the first time in years tonight. What was different?"

"The fact he didn't run off before I arrived," she replied dryly.

"But think for a second. Why did he stay?"

"Because he got held up going out the door? The rear entrance was blocked? "

"No, I think he stayed because he saw you with another man."

"You think he was jealous?" She tilted her head in thought, then shook it. "Nope. Probably more of that misplaced big brother protection crap. He did the same thing after the prom with my poor date." She could still see it, Mitchell slugging Tommy in the face, saying over and over, "You dirty pig. Keep your hands off my sister."

"I think Mitchell is mistaken in his feelings. I say, we test him."

"What exactly are you suggesting?" she asked.

"We date." At her arched brown, he added. "Pretend date. We'll need to enlist Naomi's help. She'll find out where Mitchell is going to be, and we'll show up looking like a happy couple."

"And he breathes a great big sigh of relief because he thinks I don't want him."

"Or, if he's truly your mate, he won't be able to help himself from trying to shove me out of the picture and claim you for himself."

She eyed him suspiciously. "And what do you get out of this?"

"A place to stay. A chance to needle my brother, among others. And in the pursuit of our answer to Mitchell's affection, make-out time with a hot redhead."

Her lips quirked. "Anyone ever tell you that you're an evil, evil man?"

"All the time, usually followed by handcuffs." Laughter spilled from her, which he joined, his low tenor doing strange things to her insides.

Oh God, she'd have to lock her door tonight, and then toss the key so she didn't come back down to ravage him. Despite her feelings for Mitchell, she couldn't deny Alejandro made her hot—soaking wet, smoldering pussy, hot.

Chapter Four

Alejandro tossed and turned on the couch after Francine went to bed. What had possessed him to ask her to pretend date him? And so she could snag that idiot wolf! The lady deserved better than some dog who lacked the ability to recognize the true beauty right in front of him. If it were him, he'd fall to his knees and worship the fiery goddess who could moan so deliciously.

God, when she'd faked that orgasm, Alejandro almost leapt over the counter, ready to bend her over and sink his cock into her pussy. More shocking, his cat almost made him follow his visual fantasy, but with one added element, his teeth sinking into her flesh and marking her.

She's not meant for me. Or so he kept telling himself as he shifted position, trying to ignore his rigid cock. The willpower it took not to follow her upstairs, or beg for a kiss, almost killed him. He'd never felt a desire this fierce before, and he'd never had to fight his beast for control.

Could she be the one? He knew his father scoffed at Javier's choice to remain true to one woman, preferring to spread his love around, even as he always returned to his and Javier's mother. It drove them nuts that she accepted their father's wandering ways, especially when they saw the sadness in her eyes as she learned of a new conquest or child he'd fathered. Alejandro always swore he'd never do the same. He never made any promises to a woman, nor did he leave a trail of bastards behind. That way no one got hurt.

Of course, that plan didn't always work with some women getting attached without his meaning to. And that, in turn, led to irate fathers hunting him down, usually with a shotgun, trying to force a mating or marriage he didn't want. Hence his current visit to Javier, the length of which still remained to be determined. He'd done more this time than bed the wrong girl. He'd come to the attention of the wrong father, a hunter who'd unfortunately clued in to his heritage. Oops.

Maybe it's time I changed towns for good. This seems like a nice place, and I've got my brother, as well as some nieces or nephews on the way. His mother would miss him, but truly, the woman had her hands full with his other siblings and probably wouldn't miss the drama that came with having him around.

And his decision to stay for a while certainly had nothing to do with a short and curvy redhead who pretended not to want him while her scent screamed arousal.

Fuck, he needed to get a handle on his lust. Sticking his hand under the blanket, naked as per habit, he grabbed his thick cock. His erection hadn't fully died since he'd met the fiery little wolf, and he couldn't go on with it constantly pointing in her direction.

Up and down, he stroked it, the blanket getting caught up in his fisting. With a growl, he kicked the cover off, the air of the room not cooling his skin down one bit. One leg braced on the floor, the other bent on the couch, he resumed his masturbation, his hand moving with an even cadence on his engorged shaft.

Despite himself, he couldn't help imagining Francine as he touched himself, a delightful vision of her on her knees, her sweet brown eyes peering up at him as she licked his cock, making him groan aloud. He could so easily imagine her red curls bouncing as she blew him, her perfect lips stretched around his girth, her cheeks hollowing. Caught up in his fantasy, he almost missed the small gasp from behind him where the stairway hid in shadows. Not letting on that he knew she'd come down, he continued to stroke his cock, thrusting his hips up, and biting back a smile as her scent, musky with arousal, drifted to him.

He dared not say a word or show any sign that he knew of her presence. It would send her fleeing for sure. However, knowing she couldn't help watching…God, he couldn't help grunting as he quickened his pace. Say what you would, having an audience always made things more erotic. When he caught her own breathing coming just as fast as his, he didn't bother holding back. He came, his hot cream spurting onto his belly, the relief pleasant but nothing compared to coming inside a woman's body.

Taking his time standing, he made sure to not turn around before he'd heard her scurry back up the stairs. His own chivalry surprised him, but something about Francine screamed he not push her, even if he just planned to have casual sex. As he washed up, it occurred to him to wonder if she hid under her covers, playing with herself, aroused at his show. His cock immediately hardened as if he'd never touched it.

Naked still, and now curious, he snuck up her stairs and crept to her door. He hovered, listening. Silence, though, hung thick, and he held back a sigh. *I guess she went to sleep.*

Just as he turned to leave though, he heard her speak. "You took too long. I'm done, and might I say, thank you for the visual stimulation. It really helped *grease* things along." She giggled, then laughed like a mad woman when he growled and stomped back down the stairs.

Little brat. If he'd known she would just use him to get herself off, he'd have… *What? Invited her to join me? Joined her?* Either way, they'd both used each other to masturbate. It just miffed him that for the first time he could recall, a woman didn't need him to achieve orgasm. Talk about throwing the gauntlet down, and dammit, she couldn't have done a worse thing, because now, he'd have to bed her. His ego demanded it, as did his cock.

Chapter Five

Coward, I'm a bloody coward. Francine couldn't deny the truth when she found herself unable to leave her bedroom the next morning, her brazenness of the night before melted with daylight and the knowledge Alejandro waited below.

When she'd come down the night before for a glass of milk, she'd never expected to find her guest fisting himself on the couch. Even more shocking, she'd found herself riveted by his display. A proper young lady would have run back up the stairs and slammed her door shut to show him what she thought of his dirty act on her couch. Of course, Francine had missed getting the handbook on how a lady should behave, so instead, she stood and watched. Stared actually, panting softly as he stroked a thick, hard cock that would have looked so much better buried inside her pussy.

Dammit all, It made her horny, enough that she forgot the milk and scurried back to her room. She'd no sooner closed her door than she ripped off her jammies and rubbed her clit. Lubed and excited already, she'd come quick, gasping and arching on her bed to the mental vision of Alejandro sucking her tits while he fucked her. Such a bad girl—and an unexpectedly erotic visual—but damn, did she enjoy it.

As her breathing calmed, she'd heard Alejandro arrive to spy on her. Pig. Funny thing was, had he arrived a minute before, she might have flung the door open and dragged him in, so overcome was she with lust. Instead, feeling more in control now that she'd climaxed, she taunted the man who'd thrown her carefully—sometimes crazy—ordered plan to claim Mitchell in disarray. How dare he make her desire him? How dare he make her so hot, she pumped her hand like a wild bitch in heat?

She could almost see his shock as she told him what she'd done then giggled. God, she'd enjoyed that. But that was last night. Day arrived along with a need to get up, dress, and go to work. She'd used her ensuite to shower and dress, hoping he'd leave while she got ready, but judging by the music and movement she heard from below, he'd not gotten the hint.

Sighing, she mentally slapped herself for acting like a ninny and opened the door. *This is my house, and he's just a guy, albeit a hot fucking one. If he says anything to embarrass me, I'll sic Naomi on him.* Decided, she marched downstairs, her nose twitching as she caught the smell of pancakes and bacon. *He cooked?*

Incredulous, she went into the kitchen and saw two plates heaped with pancakes and bacon waiting on her breakfast counter.

"About time you showed up, sleepy head," Alejandro said, turning from the stove with a grin that made her heart lurch. He expertly flipped another pancake onto a plate. "I would hate to make a pig of myself and eat this all alone."

"Morning. And thanks."

"For breakfast? My pleasure, baby."

"No, although that's nice, I meant for helping me relax so I could get a good night's sleep." Why she brought it up after agonizing upstairs over what to say, she'd never know. Cheeks heating, she took a seat at a stool. She grabbed her fork and dug in, keeping a wary eye on him as she waited for him to reply and make a comment of his own about the previous night. Actually, looking forward to it so she could get indignant—or saucy. However, he ate in silence, only his eyes occasionally paying her attention, the mischievous light in them the only indication that he'd guessed her thoughts.

"So, what are your plans for the day?" she asked in between bites, breaking the silence.

"After I take you to work, I'm going to go by my brother's place and grab my bags. I'd already offloaded them from the bike when you invited me to stay."

A decision she now wondered about. Should she tell him she'd changed her mind? That he had to leave because she didn't trust herself alone with him? Glancing at his smirk, she could tell he waited for her to do just that. Ha, like he'd win that easily.

"Perfect. Don't forget to grab some groceries too while you're out then. I'd hate for us to go *hungry*. I wouldn't mind some sausage, long and thick for me sink my teeth in. A nice juicy hunk of meat, the kind that you can slap between some toasted, yet soft in the middle buns. Ooh and some popsicles. I do so love to suck on them when I'm hot. And cream, lots of cream." She managed not to grin as his eyes went slightly out of focus at her innuendos.

Alejandro groaned and banged his head off the counter muttering, "And my brother was worried about me taking advantage of you. You're a cruel, cruel woman."

"What? What did I say?" she exclaimed, pretending innocence. She couldn't hold onto her placid demeanor, and burst into giggles that made his lips twitch.

"I'll get you back," he warned, clearing the breakfast dishes. "And when I do, you won't be laughing, screaming maybe, and soaking wet, but definitely no giggling."

"I'm taken," she gasped between snorts, unable to stop her body from reacting to his promise.

"Oh, you'll be taken all right," he leered.

"Pig."

"Tease."

They grinned at each other and burst into laughter, sharing a strange rapport similar to the one she owned with Naomi. *Except I've never wanted to give my BFF a blow job followed by a good fuck.*

"So you giving me a *ride* to work?" she asked, arching a brow.

"You are going to kill me, I swear," he grumbled good-naturedly as he stalked off to grab his jacket.

"Does that mean you don't intend to help with the plan to make Mitchell jealous?" she called after him, wondering if she'd pushed him too far. She liked his idea of making Mitchell take note of her, and if she'd admit it to herself, she liked Alejandro. He made her laugh, and for a lighthearted person like herself, that rocked. If the plan to get

Mitchell failed, perhaps Alejandro would make a good backup. Then she mentally slapped herself.

Alejandro chased anything in a skirt. Sure, she posed a challenge since she'd not fallen onto his prick with the first smile, but once she let him conquer her pussy, he'd move on. It was what men like him did. So setting her sights on him as some type of second place prize seemed foolish. Although, using him to console her bruised heart, and aching cleft, would maybe work.

Great, I've got one man who doesn't want me, and another who wants me until he gets me.

As if he read her mind, Alejandro came back and said, "You won't get rid of me that easily, baby. Now get that hot ass of yours outside and on that bike before I decide we should practice playing the happy couple on your couch—naked."

The smoldering look in his eyes had her scurrying even as interest moistened her pussy. Damn, but the man tore at her defenses. If only he'd come along before her plan to finally win Mitchell over. She'd have had him naked and feasting between her thighs. Yum.

This plan better work because I'm going to need some sexual relief soon in a bad way. And somehow, she doubted there were enough batteries in the world to keep her vibrator going long enough to put out the fire in her sex.

* * * *

Driving with the sexy wolf on the back of his bike was pure torture. It didn't help he had to stuff his hard-on into his leather pants of the day before. And unfortunately for him, jerking off in the shower that morning before she came down hadn't made the situation any better, not when he kept replaying her words of the night before. So much for thinking of her as a sweet, delicate thing. She still appeared it, but owned a delightful potty mouth that could drop a man to his knees. And she knew it too. Brat.

Much as he ached from wanting to have her—naked in a variety of positions—he couldn't deny how much he also enjoyed her presence and quick wit. He'd rarely come across a woman who could resist him when he poured on the charm. More intriguing, he could tell she desired him. She couldn't completely hide the scent of her lust or the bright hunger in her eyes. And yet, she seemed to have no problem keeping him at bay, and her hands to herself. Such a shame, which of course was why he didn't tell her that her car was returned that morning in perfect working condition. He'd parked it around the corner on purpose because he wanted her wrapped around his body on the bike, her squeals of excitement a cheap thrill. He also kept hoping she'd let her hands stray south to the juncture of his thighs so she could see how she affected him, but while she clutched him tight, her hands never strayed from his chest. A pity.

When they arrived at her workplace, she hopped off and removed his helmet, handing it to him. He ignored it and snagged her with one hand before she could walk away.

"Did you want something?" she asked, laughter dancing in her eyes, her lips curving into a sensual smile that did crazy things to his heart.

A need to taste those lips made him think fast. "Well, if I'm not mistaken, you work with shifters, and some of them might know Mitchell. We wouldn't want them to report back that we parted without a single kiss. We are, after all, supposed to be playing the part of the happy couple."

"I think you're just looking for an excuse to grope me," she replied, seeing right through his ruse, but she didn't attempt to pull away.

"Who, me?" He widened his eyes in false innocence and grinned as he reeled her in until his thigh slid between her legs. "Now would I take advantage of the situation to kiss a gorgeous woman?"

"No. You're much too chivalrous for that," she sighed in mock resignation. "But I'm not."

She leaned in and pressed her mouth to his, a soft, fleeting touch that sent tingles through him, and made him crave more. When she would have pulled away, though, attempting to keep their embrace fleeting, he tightened his arm around her body, anchoring her in place. Then he kissed her back, allowing some of his restrained passion to break free.

Lightning struck, leaving him dazed, but even in his befuddled state, which had his cat yeowling, he remembered how to move his mouth against hers. To grasp her lower lip between his and suck on it until she panted. A sane man would have broken off the kiss at that point, but unfortunately all reason seemed to have fled him. He didn't stop, instead, he pressed his hard thigh against her core, which straddled him, and licked the seam of her mouth, tasting her.

Need her. Need to claim her. Fuck her. Mark her. Oh shit.

Before he could bend her over and take her, damn anybody watching, he released her, and she stumbled back. God, she looked so beautiful with her face flushed, lips swollen, and he could hear her heart pounding even over her huffing breath. He wanted to drag her back to him. Kiss her again. Take her somewhere and make love to her until her nails raked his back and she begged him to mark her. To keep her forever.

I am in so much fucking trouble. "See you in a little while," he managed to say through his growing panic. It killed him to ignore the disappointment that clouded her expression along with the confusion—and lust, lust for him, not Mitchell.

Straightening her spine, she threw him a feeble smile. "Well, that wasn't so bad. At least I don't want to throw up like I did with Ken a few years back. Of course, in his defense, I'd downed a lot of Sex On The Beach shooters. But next time, mind groping me a little more? No one's ever going to believe we're madly passionate about each other with your hands not even grabbing my ass. I mean, seriously. You'll have to do better."

And before he could drag his fiery brat back to prove he'd restrained himself, she sauntered off, that pert, rounded backside of hers swaying hypnotically.

Yup, so completely and utterly fucked. And yet, despite the dawning realization that Francine might end up being more than a quick screw, he couldn't help smiling. Because, after all, she'd kissed him…and liked it despite her words. The damp spot on his leather pants said so.

* * * *

Mitchell stalked over to his sister's bright and early the next morning, having prepared his speech to Javier's brother a good part of the night. When he entered Naomi's bright kitchen and saw her sitting, having breakfast with only her two mates, he didn't immediately clue in that Alejandro never returned the night before. Never mind the fact he'd heard Francine's invitation for the cat to sleep on her couch. As a good girl, he knew she'd come to her senses and send the Casanova on his way.

Addressing Javier, he said in his man of the family voice, "I need to speak to your brother about Francine."

Naomi arched a brow. "Excuse me, but what happened to hello, how are you feeling today? Or how about the basics, like knocking? Did someone get up on the wrong side of the bed today? Because I somehow doubt Alejandro did." Then she snickered, and her meaning filtered up to his brain, making a red haze drop over his gaze.

"You mean that little pervert actually spent the night at Francine's?" he roared. "How you could you let him defile her? She's your best friend."

He'd no sooner spoken than a bristling Javier stood before him. "Watch your tone. The pervert you are speaking of is my brother. And Francine is the one who invited him to stay on her couch."

"I thought she said that last night just to piss me off. You mean he actually stayed?"

"Yes. Is that a problem, Mitchell?" his sister asked, calmly buttering some toast. "After all, it's not like you own her or anything. Francine is free to see anyone she likes. And I like Alejandro. He's cute." A growl sounded and she added, "Although not as cute as my mates, who apparently need reminding still after last night."

Ethan dropped his head and blushed, Javier grinned, and Mitchell groaned. "Oh gross, Naomi. I so don't need that kind of mental image."

"Fine, then picture Francine and Alejandro instead. Personally, I think they'd make pretty babies and since you're not going to give them to her, she might as well go for cute."

"But he's a—a—"

"What? Seducer of women? Lover with excellent technique? Good-looking bastard?" Alejandro wandered in and grinned at them all, looking entirely too smug. "Yes to all of the above. Morning, everyone. Isn't it a glorious morning? Much as I'd like to stay and discuss how beautiful any babies Francine and I make would be, I just came to grab my saddlebags. I'm going to need some changes of clothing while I'm staying with Francine."

"How dare you take advantage of her? You need to go to a motel or something," Mitchell blurted.

"Why, when the accommodation I have is so...what's the word I'm looking for? Oh yes, sumptuous." Alejandro leered, and Mitchell's traitorous sister giggled.

"Keep your hands off her." He almost ground his teeth to dust so tightly did he clench his jaw.

"Why should I? She's unclaimed, beautiful and best of all, has a wonderful mind and quick wit."

"Are you trying to tell me you're her mate?" Mitchell almost choked on the question as his wolf snarled in his mind, not at all enthralled with the idea of another touching Francine.

"Let me see," Alejandro said, tapping his chin. "She makes my cat meow, which I admit is quite distracting. She makes my cock harder than a bar of steel. Oh, and I could listen to her for hours, screaming that is, as I fuck her."

As red flags went, that one was a doozy. Mitchell dove at him as Naomi shouted, "Not in my house. Ethan, do something!"

One good swing was all he managed, and it missed, before Ethan grabbed him, pinning his arms back as Alejandro regarded him smugly until Javier cuffed him in the back of the head.

"Hey," the seducer exclaimed.

"Stop baiting him. Mitchell, ignore my brother. He's got no interest in Francine. He's just trying to piss you off. It's what he excels at."

"I resent that," said the dead man walking indignantly.

"But it's true."

"Oh, I don't mean the pissing off part. I don't deny it. But I'll have you know, I am very interested in Francine. Enough, that I am going to do something I've never done before," Alejandro announced. "I am taking her on a date."

Shocked silence met his words. Javier whispered, "Oh my God. He's serious. Naomi, you have to stop him. If he gets with Francine then that means he'll never leave, and I'll have to put up with him—" Javier gulped. "Almost daily."

His sister, who'd crossed over to the enemy's side, clapped her hands. "Ooh, that would be awesome. I've always thought Alejandro was the most fun of your brothers. And it means, even though Mitchell wouldn't step up to the plate, she'll still end up my sister-in-law."

"Thanks, Naomi," beamed the interloper. "Your blessing means a lot to me. Now, if you'll excuse me, I need to grab my stuff and change so I can meet with up with Francine for lunch. It's a surprise date." Whistling, Alejandro wandered off, and Ethan released Mitchell.

Scowling, Mitchell said, "You're not seriously going to condone this, are you?"

"Why Mitchell, if I didn't know better, I'd say you're jealous. Are you?" All three of them stared at him as they awaited his answer.

The word "Yes!" almost slipped past his lips. He bit his tongue. Growling, he turned on his heel and left without answering. *I'm not jealous, just watching out for Francine since no one else seems willing to.* He kept repeating that lie to himself as he grabbed a quick shower and change of clothes of his own before he jumped in his car and headed to Francine's work, not even coming close to obeying speed limits. The location of her employment, which he'd previously not given a damn about, he pried out of his mother. His mama had given him a hard look when he asked, along with a terse, "Why?"

His reply to something he couldn't even explain to himself? "Because." And that was all he'd said. His mother snorted at his one word reply, but gave him the address to Francine's work anyway and said she hoped he'd come to his senses.

Actually, Mitchell felt like he'd lost part of his mind, but he didn't care. Only one thing drove him at this point, keeping Francine from making a colossal mistake. Not because he planned to date or claim her. She was still his honorary sister, but as her honorary older brother, it behooved him to keep her from suave kitties out to get in her pants and break her heart.

I'm doing her a favor. She'll thank me for it later. It made him almost groan aloud when his mind flashed a picture of her on her knees thanking him orally. *I so need to get laid. Tonight, after I deal with this mess, I'll call Jenny,* his on-and-off-again girlfriend. Problem was, he couldn't even picture the blonde woman he'd known intimately for years. Francine's face kept superimposing itself over it. He didn't quite understand what drove him to imagine the forbidden, what madness currently controlled him. An urge to protect Francine he understood, but the rest, the rage when thinking of her with Alejandro, the strange lust when he recalled her grown up appearance, it didn't make sense.

The reaction of his wolf he especially found baffling because it snarled and paced in his mind, urging him to do something, but Mitchell ignored it. *I mean, biting Francine just to keep her from that seducer? That's just crazy. I'll deal with this like I always do, by ordering her away, and if that fails, my fists getting up close and personal with that bastard's face.* He kind of hoped he'd have to indulge in the latter.

Bringing his car to a stop front of the office building his mother directed him to, he angled in to a metered spot. He parked and grinned, possibly a little like a maniac, when he didn't notice a bike, which meant he'd beat the cat here.

But he had to hurry if he planned to get her out of there for their talk before the seducer arrived. Of course, when he saw her, sitting, looking so prim and proper at her desk, wild red hair tamed into a bun, typing away, his first thought wasn't his prepared for-your-own-good speech. No, instead, he wondered if she'd wear that intent look while he fucked her, spread out on that desk, papers flying.

He almost slapped himself. *Wrong. So wrong. Remember, she's like a sister. Not cute and delicious-looking at all.*

Forcing himself to remember that, and his purpose for coming, he bore down on her, using angry thoughts to distract him from naked ones.

* * * *

It was her wolf that sensed him first, yipping in her head that she had company. Francine looked up from her desk to see a grim-faced Mitchell bearing down on her. Despite his unpleasant expression, a flutter of anticipation made her heart beat faster.

"We're going to lunch," he announced, not sounding at all pleased by the prospect.

"Gee, thanks for asking," she replied dryly. "Did you turn into a caveman overnight? Or do simple manners elude you?" She couldn't help the sarcasm even if he'd finally asked her out. For some reason, when she'd imagined their first date, he'd looked a lot happier about it.

Ruddy color rose in his cheeks. "Sorry. I'm, uh, hungry. That's it, hungry, and I was in the area and thought I'd ask if you'd like to join me."

Something didn't seem right. She peered out of the window, examining the sky, and didn't answer.

Her lack of response made him fidget. "Um, Francine, what are you doing?"

"I don't have a direct line to hell to see if it's frozen over so I'm looking for flying pigs."

"What's that supposed to mean?"

"It means you've ignored me like I had some contagious disease for the last five years and now all of a sudden, in the last twenty-four hours, you're constantly in my face. Mind telling me what's up?" She turned back to stare at him, trying not to grin at how uncomfortable he seemed.

"Can't a man ask an old friend to lunch?" he grumbled, looking so adorably flustered that she wanted to jump up and kiss him silly. Then slap him for being such an ass.

"I guess," she said, still wondering what prompted his impromptu visit. She and Alejandro hadn't even put their plan in motion. Was it working already? *Maybe someone did report the kiss. Talk about news traveling quick.*

"Good, then get your purse so we can go."

Standing, she went to the filing cabinet to grab it from the drawer she kept it stashed in. "What's the hurry? You on your lunch break too?"

"Not exactly. I've actually got the week off. The office is getting repainted." Working as a sales rep, of all things, for a human corporation specializing in heating and cooling services, Mitchell made a decent living even if his choice of careers seemed odd. "Can you move a little faster? Please."

Biting her lip, Francine fought not to laugh at this frantic Mitchell who'd gone out of his way to invite her to lunch. Perhaps the tides had turned and the mating fever had finally snagged him. Talk about wishful thinking.

Mitchell didn't say another word as she followed him to the elevator and down to the lobby. Actually, he actively avoided meeting her gaze, which allowed her to drink in the sight of his body, a hot bod that she had only caught brief glimpses in the past few years.

His worn t-shirt hugged his wiry frame, the soft material stretching across his broad shoulders. Well-washed jeans clung to his thighs, the waist of them hanging low on lean hips. His hair stood in untamed tufts as if he'd run his fingers through it. As for his face, he still sported the same sharp-angled features, piercing eyes, and square chin. Ruggedly handsome as ever.

While she let herself drink in the sight of him, he kept his gaze pointed squarely at her feet clad in low heels that she kept stashed at the office. She'd also thankfully had a spare set of clothes because Alejandro had left the crotch in her first pair of pants ridiculously wet after his kiss. The pig. Speaking of whom, she wondered what he did while Mitchell escorted her to lunch.

It was as they exited through the glass doors at the front that she saw the object of her thoughts and caught Mitchell's triumphant grin. Oh, how nice. She'd gotten caught in the middle of a male pissing contest. Good thing she'd learned to aim years ago from the numerous times she went camping, because she couldn't wait to join in.

"Jag," she cried out, waving.

"Jag?" Mitchell growled.

At Mitchell's pointed glare, she smiled. "His name is so long to pronounce, especially in the heat of the moment, that I gave him a shorter one that went well I thought with his great, big, powerful beast. Don't worry, Mitchy," she said, using the nickname he'd hated as a kid, which she'd not thought about in years. "I won't ditch you for lunch. You did, after all, ask me first. You don't mind if Jag joins us, do you? He did, after all, go out of his way just to see me. Besides, I'm sure if you give each other a chance, you'll find you have loads in common."

She didn't have time to enjoy Mitchell's open mouthed incredulity for long because she found herself spun and a pair of lips plastered to hers. Oh, how nice that felt. Like that morning, when he'd insisted on a kiss, tingles shot through her body and she lost her breath at the excitement his simple touch ignited. She didn't want to analyze her reaction to him too closely, but she began to fear that despite her affection and longing for Mitch, Alejandro might also play a part in her future mating plans. *I'll have to kiss Mitch too, though, to be sure. I wonder if I can convince him to let me?*

She didn't get to enjoy the embrace for long as Jag, in full fake boyfriend mode, lifted his head and smiled down at her with all the lazy grace of a cat who'd caught the canary. "Hey, baby. I wanted to surprise you and take you out to for something meaty to eat."

"Mmm, sounds delicious," she purred back. "You don't mind if Mitchy comes along, do you? He was in the area and asked me first. And he's awfully grumpy, apparently, when he's hungry."

"Not a problem. My mama always did teach me to share." And then, he winked at Mitchell.

For a moment, she thought for sure Mitchell would either blow his top or die of embarrassment at Alejandro's sly innuendo.

Instead, he tightened his lips and said through gritted teeth, "Let's go."

It was a good thing Alejandro had a good grip on her hand to guide her along because she'd completely gone blank at Alejandro's mention of sharing. It made her instantly picture both of them with her, pleasing her. What a shame Mitchell would never go for it, especially since the more time she spent with them both, her wolf spinning, her heart racing, and her cleft soaking, the more she wondered what she would do if she had to choose. Would she pick the man she'd known and loved forever who kept denying her, or the Casanova she'd just met who said all the right things and made no bones about the fact he desired her, but who would likely leave once the novelty wore off?

From no men to too many. Fate truly liked messing with people.

Sitting between them in a u-shaped booth at a nearby sports bar with great food, she glanced back and forth at them, not that they noticed, too intent were they on glaring at each other. Actually, Mitchell glared, Alejandro smirked. Apparently, she'd have to get the conversational ball rolling while trying avoid a bar fight. What fun.

"So, Mitchell, why exactly did you seek me out for lunch?"

"Yeah, Mitchy," Alejandro teased, grasping her hand to lace his fingers through it. "I have to say, if I'd known we were going to have a third wheel, I'd have brought the lube."

A tic formed in Mitchell's temple and he gritted his teeth. "First off, I'm not here to have sex with Francine. Or with you, you disgusting pervert."

Alejandro laughed. "Oh, the lube wasn't for you, but my sweet wolf here. Nothing like a sandwich to get a woman screaming, in pleasure, of course. Don't worry, I have no designs on your scrawny body. Francine's though…" He turned to look at her, and shot her a sultry smile as he stroked his thumb over the skin of her hand.

A shiver went through her and heat pooled in her cleft. It didn't help that now she couldn't help imagining herself naked between two male bodies. So not happening despite her curiosity. Mitchell would cut off his dick to spite them first. Besides, she couldn't even seem to convince Mitch to do her, so forget convincing him to share her with another. At the rate this conversation went, she'd probably end up humping her hand alone again because they'd both end up in the hospital, victims of male arrogance and testosterone.

Despite knowing Alejandro's suggestion would never bear fruit, she played along anyways. The entertainment value was just too good to pass up. "Jag!" she squealed. "You naughty, naughty man. What a fun idea, but Mitchy isn't into doing wild and kinky stuff, though. He's more of a missionary man, so I hear. Aren't you, Mitchell?" She smiled at him serenely, biting the inside of her cheek so as to not laugh at his red-faced, glowering expression. *I am so bad for teasing him.* But then again, she wasn't about to change her nature for anyone, not even Mitchell. Raunchiness and outrageous comments were her forte.

"I'm not a prude," he muttered through gritted teeth.

Patting his hand, she cajoled him. "Sure you aren't. It's okay, not everyone is into sexual experimentation."

"Or extreme pleasure, apparently," Alejandro said, tilting her chin so she gazed his way. And oh, if she didn't know he played a part, she would have swooned at the heat in his eyes. The promise in his sensual lips…

A growl startled her from her eye contact with Alejandro, and she turned to glance at Mitchell. Still ruddy-cheeked, his eyes blazed while his hands on the table were clenched into white-knuckled fists. "Enough. Francine. You can't seriously tell me you're actually dating this guy? Not only is he a pervert, he's a womanizing pig."

"Cat."

"Whatever, asshole. Anyone can see he's just going to break your heart."

"Like you haven't?" she replied tartly.

That made him squirm and drop his gaze. "I never made any promises to you. You were the one chasing me. I tried to let you down easy."

For some reason, that pissed her off. Yes, she'd chased him, but how dare he make her sound like some desperate bitch. She'd only gone after him because her instincts said he belonged to her. "I see. Well, consider me let down, Mitchell. You were right. I can't force you to love me. Or care for me or even want me. Alejandro, on the other hand, does. So congrats, you're free. I'm done letting a foolish girlhood fantasy dictate my life."

Opening and shutting his mouth a few times, Mitchell seemed at a loss for words. "So that's it? You don't think we're meant to be mates anymore?"

Actually, she knew the exact opposite, and her inner wolf howled in frustration that he didn't see it too. "Oh, I know you're supposed to be mine. Even now my wolf is telling me to pounce on you and sink my teeth in. But don't worry," she said, shaking her head sadly when he leaned away from her. "It's obvious you don't feel the same way. And besides, it looks like fate's found you a replacement." She turned away from Mitchell, her heart heavy that she'd bared it all and he still insisted they weren't meant to be. Alejandro slid on the bench until he could curl his arm around her. She welcomed his warmth and turned into him, nuzzling the skin of his neck.

"I'm sorry, Francine," Mitch whispered. "I—um—that is, you're like a—"

She tensed. "I know. I know. I'm like a sister to you. Bye, Mitchell. You don't need to hide anymore. I'm done."

Forcing herself to not look at him as he left, she instead inhaled Alejandro's scent, its muskiness exciting and soothing at the same time. Her wolf paced in her mind, confused. On the one paw, it wanted her to not let Mitchell, who stood with a rustle, walk away. But at the same time, her inner bitch wanted her to open her mouth wide and put her mark on the tanned column before her. Claim this man who'd made her no promises and simply played a convincing role, one that fooled even her human side so sincere did he appear.

"He's gone," murmured Alejandro. "He's a fucking idiot, you know."

Trying to move away from temptation, she found herself unable to, Alejandro's arm anchoring her at his side.

"He's not an idiot, just too honorable. Kind of like you, I think."

"Me?" Incredulous eyes peered down at her. "I've been called a lot of things in my life, baby, but honorable? Not even close."

"Perhaps because you've never had an opportunity. I think you're a lot more chivalrous than you give yourself credit for."

He dropped a kiss on the tip of her nose. "And you are lucky we are in a public place or I'd show you just how non principled I am."

"Mmm, public sex. That's not a threat," she purred. "That's foreplay." Down went his head onto the table with a thump while Francine laughed. "Was it something I said?"

"When I agreed to this ruse," he mumbled, his face still buried. "I didn't expect you to try and kill me by making my blue balls explode."

"Poor Jag. Am I too much for you to handle? It wouldn't be the first time a man's had that problem. Hell, the prime example just walked away. Speaking of which, our target's gone so you don't need to pretend anymore."

Turning his head sideways, Alejandro's dark eyes regarded her with a seriousness she found disturbing. "And what if it weren't an act for his benefit? What if I did feel something for you? What would you say?"

His words took her by surprise, especially since she'd thought them herself. Did she want Alejandro as a lover? *Yes.* Did she want him forever? *Too soon to know.* Did she still want Mitchell? *Damn me, I still do.*

An answer to his question didn't arrive before their waitress did with drinks, and seeing the way she smiled coyly and flirted with Alejandro reminded Francine of one important fact. *He's a lady's man. Even if he finds me intriguing now, how can I throw away a possibility with Mitchell, knowing full well Alejandro will probably walk once I give in to his charm?*

Sliding away from him, trying to regain some sense of equilibrium, they ordered. As they waited for their food, she analyzed the Mitchell thing while skipping the whole feeling thing she'd discovered for Alejandro. She didn't want to get into the fact that everything she'd said about him was true and not a script for their plot.

Alejandro abruptly broke the silence. "Jag, huh? Nice spur of the minute thinking. Is it short for my cat? The mighty black jaguar, feared by all."

She giggled. "Nope. For some reason, you make me think of a cocky air force pilot, which in turn, made me think of the military, and that show Jag. But, I guess it does work both ways."

He clasped his chest. "Ooh, take a man down a notch why don't you."

"My grandmas taught me well."

"You're close to them?"

"Very," she said, stirring her drink. "They both pretty much raised me."

"What about your parents, or is that topic off limits?"

"I've got nothing to hide." Other than the fact Mitchell wasn't the first to walk away from her, tearing her heart in the process. "My mom got pregnant in her teens with another shifter. Neither was ready to settle down or deal with the responsibility of a child. So I spent my time going back and forth between my grandparents' houses. Heck, even now my mom can't be bothered to remember she has a child. She's off on some cruise somewhere with her newest boyfriend. As for my dad, I haven't seen him in years. Last I heard, he was living in the Bahamas with his latest girlfriend."

Eyes of melted chocolate peered at her with a hint of sadness. "That sucks."

She shrugged. It had, but she'd gotten over it—mostly. "I met Naomi while staying at my maternal grandmother's place. My grandma would go over for coffee with Meredith, Naomi's mom, and even though we were babies, we hit it off."

"I bet the pair of you caused all kinds of havoc."

A giggle worked its way past her lips. "Oh my God, did we ever. I don't think Chris ever forgave us for pinning him down and dressing him in a diaper so we could use him as a real baby to play house."

Alejandro winced. "Okay, now you're making me glad I never had sisters."

"You missed out then," she said with a grin. "What about your family? Javier's never talked about it much other than to say his brothers are pains in the asses and that your mother is a saint."

A twinkle appeared in his eyes. "Who, us? And he's right, my mother is a saint. She had to be. There's five of us boys in total. We just about drove her insane with our antics."

"What about your dad?"

"Who knows? He flits around, leaving behind half brothers and sisters that we've never met."

"Oh. Your parents split up?"

"Not exactly. My father is not a believer in monogamy, and my mother foolishly allows him to get away with it. He goes and plays, then when he tires of it, he comes home to my mother's open arms." Alejandro's gaze dropped, but not before she saw the anger and hurt in his eyes. It seemed her Jag didn't agree with his father's philosophy. A point in his favor.

Francine's lips tightened. "I'd never tolerate that."

"And yet you see no problem with Naomi's situation?" He teased her, but she defended her words anyway.

"There's a difference in several people choosing to live in a polyamorous relationship, who are committed to each other only. It's a whole other thing for someone to go chasing after other people to have sex while hurting the family they have." It came out a little more vehemently than she meant, but she hated the obvious pain he felt at the way his father treated their mother.

"I agree with you one hundred percent."

She blinked. "You do?"

"You don't hurt the people you love, ever. Sex, after all, is only a fleeting pleasure."

"And yet you seem to engage in lots of it," she replied dryly.

"Only because none of my partners ever truly made it past my body to see the man. If the right lady were to come along…"

"You'd fall hard like Javier did. I hope you find her one day," she said softly, even as a part of her screamed—and her wolf howled— that he already had.

"Maybe I have."

Not daring to look at him, scared of what she'd see, or not, she needed to change the direction of the conversation. "Well, even if your dad is a wanderer, at least you still have your mom and siblings. I'd love to belong to a big family. Not that my grandmas weren't great. But, by the time I came along, they were old, and didn't quite know what to do with me. Having Naomi and her family take me in and make me feel like one of them helped." It made her feel like she mattered.

"And thus did your crush on Mitchell begin. It makes sense."

A frown creased her brow. "It's more than a crush. He's my mate. Just ask my freakn' wolf."

He lifted his hands in a gesture of surrender. "I believe you."

Her shoulders slumped. "He doesn't. What do you think? He walked away pretty easy. Maybe he's right and I'm wrong. After all, how would I know what the mating fever feels like?"

"You'd know."

"You've felt it?" Strangely, knowing that roused a green jealousy in her and made her wolf's hackles rise.

"Maybe." He quirked his lips. "Or I've heard my brother describe it enough to know the signs."

A wrinkle of her nose made him chuckle. "Yeah, since she caved to her jocks, Naomi's turned into a right gusher about it, the bitch. I never thought she'd claim those two, not given her attitude on the whole mating matter. Then wham, she opened her eyes, had a few orgasms, and realized she couldn't live without them."

"It's funny how even the smartest people can refuse to see what's right in front of them."

Again, he stared at her with that intent, yet puzzled look. It almost seemed like he spoke to himself rather than her.

"Maybe I should just give up," she said with a sigh as she stirred the ice in her water glass with her straw.

"Coward. I thought you were a fighter?"

"I am, but— "

"But nothing. The battle is not over yet, baby."

The battle to win what, however? Mitchell or Alejandro? Why couldn't she have Naomi's luck and snag both? God, the fun she'd have.

She almost slammed her head down on the table herself at the thought. How she'd gone from wanting one impossible thing to two, she'd never understand. *Apparently, I'm a glutton for punishment.*

Chapter Six

Slamming his fist into Chris's nose—Mitchell's annoying younger brother—when he walked in the house probably didn't rank up there with his brightest, shining moments. But the little prick deserved it for saying, "Still didn't mark her, huh, dumbass? Maybe I'll have a go. Francine's got the sweetest ass I've ever seen." Then Chris mimed humping that invisible backside.

Mitchell flattened him, then jumped on him, their vigorous brawl bringing their mother from the kitchen. She let out a piercing whistle that separated them faster than Ethan could. No one messed with his mother. Not if they wanted to breathe.

"What are you doing, Mitchell?" his mother asked in that spooky calm voice of hers. At five feet nothing, with her arms crossed, what she lacked for in size, she made up in presence and attitude.

He hung his head, acting contrite. "Chris said something nasty about Francine."

"And? It's nothing worse than what I've heard you say about those bimbos you like to take out."

A growl rumbled from him. "It's different. Francine's—"

"Not your sister. While it was nice when you were growing up that you all felt such an urge to protect her, she's a woman now, and she is allowed to date who she wants until she settles down. Even Chris. It's not like you have a claim on her."

"You're ganging up on me too?" Mitchell exclaimed, his tone relaying the sense of betrayal he felt at her words. He'd expected her to take his side.

"Yes. This foolishness of yours has gone on long enough. Haven't you figured it out yet? You want her. It's why you keep losing your temper whenever she's mentioned."

"Like fuck I do," he lied even as the erotic images he kept having of her played through his mind.

"Don't make me get the soap, Mitchell. We both know that's not true. Not that it will matter soon. I was talking to Naomi, and it's beginning to look like you aren't the only man for her. Alejandro will probably be claiming her shortly, or as soon as she gives up her foolish notion that you're her only one."

Like fuck, he almost yelled. A hard swallow was all he could manage as Francine's words from the restaurant came back to haunt. *She's already given up on us. But that's okay, because despite what they all think, she's not mine and I'll prove it.* Tonight he would take Jenny out, a wolf like himself, whom he liked well enough. He'd take her to dinner then dancing before some naked horizontal tangoing back at her place. Fucking Jenny would put Francine back to her proper spot in his mind—and not atop his cock like he kept picturing.

* * * *

After the disturbing lunch, and a hot kiss from Alejandro that made her see stars, Francine tried to work, but visions of two men kept dancing in her head. On the one hand, Alejandro and his playacting had her in a tizzy. His kisses today left her aching and wet, especially the soft and sweet one he'd planted on her after lunch when dropping her off. What a panty-wetter.

As for Mitchell, he'd finally paid her attention and while he'd not exactly swept her up in a tidal wave of passion, she couldn't deny she had his blood stirring. *Mostly in irritation, but it's a start.*

When the phone rang, she dove on it, thankful for the distraction.

"Francine, what are you up to? Mom called and said Mitchell is just spinning and it's all because of you." Naomi didn't sound at all perturbed about her brother's mental state.

A satisfied grin curled Francine's lips. "Good. About freakn' time he noticed me."

"You mean, you did on purpose?" Naomi chortled. "Awesome."

"Maybe. Maybe not. The whole make him jealous thing was Alejandro's idea. He thinks if we pretend to be a couple and keep shoving it in Mitchell's face, he'll finally stop seeing me as his sister."

"I'd say it's working."

"A little too well," she mumbled.

"What's the problem?"

"What do you mean?" Francine played dumb.

78

"Don't start with me. I know you're not telling me something."

The problem with best friends? They could read a girl like a freakn' book. "It's gonna sound crazy."

"What is?"

For a moment, Francine struggled, the words sitting on the tip of her tongue, but she couldn't quite manage to spit them out. Somehow, saying them aloud would make it real, force her to acknowledge them and do something about it. But, hiding it seemed cowardly and Francine prided herself on never acting like a yellow belly. "I think Alejandro's my mate too."

Dead silence greeted her words.

"Naomi, are you there? Did you hear me?"

"Shit. I heard you. In fact, I kind of had a feeling that might be the case. Damn. You do know that's going to make the whole Mitchell thing harder? He's not the type to share."

"No shit. But that's not the only problem. If I'm right and Alejandro's my mate, how do I turn him into a male who's content with one pussy? He doesn't deny he's a ladies man. Why would he settle down with me? Why would either of them?" Short, curvy and outspoken for one night was one thing, but expecting it for a lifetime with one man already seemed an almost impossible challenge. Expecting it with two? What a joke.

"You listen here, Francine. You are gorgeous. Funny. Smart. And according to Mark Wilson, an animal in bed."

Francine giggled. She did tend to get enthusiastic in the bedroom. Not all men enjoyed that kind of aggressive behavior, though. "You're right. I am a prize. But still…"

"Shut up. I'm not listening to another word. Javier used to be a manwhore once upon a time, then he met me and he took to monogamy like a duck to water. So don't worry about it. If he's your mate, then he'll reform."

"But still? Two guys? What the heck would I do with them?"

"Do I really need to go into detail about my sex life? I thought you didn't want me to—"

Francine broke in hurriedly. "No, it's all right. Keep the details to yourself. I want to be able to look Ethan and Javier in the face." Besides, she said it more as a rhetorical question seeing as how polyamorous matings weren't a new thing to her. But, despite it running in her family, she'd never expected it to happen to her.

"Fine, no juicy tidbits, you chicken. But back to the whole threesome scenario, don't sweat it. Like me, it looks as if you're destined to have two men in your life. It's a no brainer, really, when you think of how awesome we both are. It's only natural we need more than one man to worship the ground we walk on. And two men in bed is so much hotter than one."

"You are so fucked."

"Yup, nightly, times two. Don't tell me you don't want the same thing? I know you do, you horny bitch, so stop the freakn' pity party and go get your men! Start with Alejandro. I get the feeling he won't take much to get in bed, and once he gets a taste of you, bam, he's yours. That is, unless you've forgotten to tell me something about your sleepover last night?"

Did masturbation count? "No, we haven't gotten naked together yet. But I have seen his cock."

"Is it—No, I better not ask. Javier will lose his mind. For a man who used to screw everything with a hole, he's got a funny jealous streak. Only Ethan doesn't count, anything else, and I'm treated to macho posturing."

"Like you don't do it on purpose to drive them nuts?"

"Of course I do. What's the fun of having two men who worship me if every now and then I don't make them green with jealousy? Besides, they like it, and the sex afterwards… Let's just say it blows the fucking mind, among other things."

"Great, make me even more jealous, bitch. So you don't think it's crazy? I should go for it? But what if—"

"Don't even say it. I tried to fight fate. It didn't work, and if I can't do it then my stupid brother sure as hell can't. I look forward to laughing like a fiend when he does fall. And as for Alejandro, I think you'll be surprised."

"What do you know?"

"Can't talk anymore. Apparently, I'm expected to make dinner for my jocks. Although it would be easier to just buy the poison and chug it direct," she hollered away from the phone's microphone.

"Anyway, the reason I called was to tell you to go to The Jungle tonight, about ninish."

"But I've got to work tomorrow."

"Suck it up, buttercup. If you plan on snagging my brother, then you need to be proactive. Mitchell's going to be there with that slut, Jenny."

"What?"

"He's trying to pretend he doesn't give a fuck by taking out the biggest whore he knows. So plan on being a little tired for work tomorrow and show up with Alejandro so you can prove him wrong."

"But—"

"No buts, well, until you get them both in your bed. Then, pour on the lube and butts away." Naomi cackled at her own poor joke as she hung up, leaving Francine bemused.

Claim them both? Could she dare even contemplate that kind of feat? Who knew? But Naomi did get one thing right. Francine was a fighter, and she didn't know how to give up without giving it her best shot first—or as she preferred, a naked tackle.

Work done, she left the office after saying goodbye to her bosses who barely looked up from their Blackberries, the workaholics. It didn't surprise her to see Alejandro already parked out front of the building, ready to take her home when she exited. Warmth imbued her and a smile tilted her lips, a welcoming grin he returned.

"Hey, baby. Miss me?" he asked, pulling her close for a hug.

"Tons and tons," she replied, realizing it was actually true.

"That's what I like to hear," he murmured, leaning his forehead against hers before dropping a kiss on her lips. Oh how she could get used to these types of sensual moments.

"What's that?" she asked, pointing to the pink helmet perched on the seat.

"If you're going to be a regular passenger, it only makes sense you have your own helmet. Read the back."

Picking it up, she spun it and then laughed. In red letters across the back was printed, "Hot Stuff."

"Awesome," she exclaimed, tickled he'd thought of her. "Thanks." She leaned up to kiss him on the cheek, but he turned and caught her mouth instead, the electric feel of his lips making her sigh in pleasure. All too quickly, he stepped back, but the glitter in his eyes let her know he found himself just as affected by the embrace.

"We can't dawdle. Much as I'd like to kiss you for hours. Supper awaits you." Putting his own helmet on first, he then swung his leg over the bike to straddle it before righting the bike and kicking the stand back.

Smooshing her new helmet onto her head, she then climbed on behind him and wrapped her arms around his torso. She'd grown to enjoy the rides on the back of his bike, her precarious perch the perfect excuse to snuggle. The rushing air and traffic noise made it impossible to hold a proper conversation, and yet, she didn't feel forgotten as every so often his hand would leave the grip of the handlebar and stroke the side of her thigh. Needless to say, it made her hyper aware of him.

Arriving at her place, she walked into a heavenly aroma and she gaped at him.

"I got the groceries this afternoon, as ordered. I made a lasagna, which is just about done. So have a seat, my working wolf, and let me serve you."

"I still can't believe you cook," she said with a smile.

"I do. Both in and out of the bedroom." He winked mischievously.

She dropped to one knee. "Marry me."

For the second time since she'd met him, Alejandro appeared lost for words. "Brat." He pulled her up from the floor and gave her a swat on the ass as he pushed her in the direction of the stairs. "Go change into something comfy while I check on things."

She needed a moment to freshen up, brush her helmet crushed hair, and wash her face, trying to cool her ardor. It didn't work, and actually got worst when she caught sight of him bustling around her kitchen. Talk about an all over tingle. Even just doing mundane things, the man made her body ache as if he'd spent hours on foreplay.

"How was your afternoon?" he asked, flashing her a white grin as he served up heaping portions of pasta and garlic bread.

"Boring. Although I did talk to Naomi." *And she told me, in not so many words, that I should jump your naked body until you concede you're mine.* The idea had merit. Not that she said it aloud.

"Mmm," he replied around a mouthful of food.

"She says Mitchell is spinning and that we need to go out dancing tonight." A part of her found it uncomfortable to even talk about Mitchell, despite their agreed upon plan. Naomi's suggestion she seduce Alejandro, and her own revelation about her feelings toward him gave her a sense of dishonesty. *Like I'm cheating on him.* He didn't seem to notice her discomfort. *Of course he doesn't, because he's just acting. As for the flirting when Mitchell's not around, I'd say that comes to him as natural as breathing.*

"Fantastic. You'll be delighted to know I am a fabulous dancer."

"I'm not," she grumbled. "This is one chubby girl who has no rhythm."

"First of all, you are not chubby. Deliciously curvy, yes," he said, tossing her a smoldering look. "Making me blue-balled with desire, definitely. Anytime you want me to prove how beautiful I find you, just let me know. My tongue is always ready for a workout."

"Pig," she muttered, trying hard not to blush. She'd not said it looking for a compliment, but holy freakn' hell, his answer went beyond making her feel good right into I-just-about-came.

"I'm a cat, my little wolf, and one who wouldn't mind licking every inch of you. Now that we've cleared up the fact you are the hottest thing in this town, let's discuss the dancing. If we are going to a techno club, then just leave it to me. I am an expert dancer probably because it's a lot like sex. You match your partner's rhythm and let your body move in time to theirs. I have a feeling you'll do just fine."

"And who says I'm good at sex?" She smirked.

A slow wink made her squirm. "A man knows."

"Oh, really? And what if I said you were wrong?"

"Is that an invitation?" He stood and moved toward her.

Flee the promise in his eyes or stay and enjoy it? Screw waiting for him to reach her, she stood and grabbed his shirt, pulling him against her.

"Feisty little thing," he murmured. "I like it." Bending his head, his hands on her waist pulled her up on tiptoe so he could kiss her. Back and forth, he rubbed his mouth against hers, sensual, silky touches that made her pant and clutch the fabric of his shirt, drawing him closer to her.

"Stop teasing," she growled, nipping at his lip.

The soft chuckle that emerged from him tickled her mouth. "But it's what I do best, baby. Now, tempting as I find you, we have to get ready to go out." He pulled back from her.

Incredulity made her stare at him. Seriously? He gave her a panty-wetting tease of a kiss then walked away? "I'm going to have a shower," she growled, stalking away from him. "Thank God I have a detachable massaging showerhead," she tossed over her shoulder.

Half a second, that's all it took for him to push her up against a wall, his hard body molded to hers, his eyes glittering down at her. "A man can only take so much, baby."

"Ditto," she replied. "Tease me and I'll tease you back."

"Is this your way of telling me you want something more? What about Mitchell?"

What about him? She loved Mitchell, wanted to spend her life with him, but she also wanted Alejandro. Wanted him to do the wicked things his grins and smoldering gaze promised. What she couldn't do was express that aloud. How could she? He'd think she was the biggest flake.

"I—"

The ring of a cell phone coming from the vicinity of his groin saved her. He cursed. "Get ready before we both forget what we're trying to accomplish."

Francine fled, her heart pounding, her pussy aching and her conviction that Alejandro belonged to her stronger than ever. Just ask her pacing wolf. At least he seemed to desire her as well, but once he had her, would he walk away? And if she did give in, would she lose her chance with Mitchell? The game she played seemed rife with risk, and the further she went, the more she realized the one who stood to lose the most was her. *And then where will I be?*

* * * *

Alejandro wanted to curse his brother out for interrupting the moment with Francine. Fleeing him, her confusion—and yes, lust— plain to see. He longed to chase after her, to make her admit she

87

wanted him. That she wanted to forget her plan with Mitchell and be with him instead.

In the space of twenty-four hours, Alejandro, ladies man and king of the one night stands, had fallen hard for a short and curvy she-wolf. And despite what he tried to tell himself, he knew with a certainty he'd rarely felt in his life that one taste would never be enough.

But how to convince her that while perhaps Mitchell was meant for her, it seemed fate had decided she'd also have another?

I could seduce her, make love to her delectable body all night long. Make her forget about going to the club. But would she resent him in the morning for ruining her chance with the idiot she'd loved so long? And by seducing her, would he perhaps drive Mitchell away forever? An interesting prospect for him, but one she might never forgive him for.

This indecision sucked, so it was with a sigh of annoyance that he answered the call on his cell.

"What?"

"Well hello to you too, little brother. Did I interrupt something?"

"I wish," he grumbled.

"Ah, is a woman finally giving you the run around? Welcome to the club. Don't forget, I was in your shoes almost a year ago so I know the feeling. I will say this, though; Naomi was worth every bit of the chase. Don't give up. If you feel that strongly about her, things will work out."

What a surreal topic of conversation, one he'd never expected to have. "It's crazy," Alejandro replied, the sound of the shower upstairs letting him know he could talk freely. "I mean, I barely know her, and yet, it's like I've known her forever. All day long, I couldn't stop thinking about her. And as for my cat… Fucking kitty is going insane in my mind, wanting to bite her and mark her. I'm afraid to shift for fear it will start pissing all over her house, leaving its scent to warn others off."

A chuckle came through the earpiece. "Sounds familiar. Don't worry, while that feeling won't go away entirely, even once you've claimed her, it will become easier to bear once you don't have to fight it."

"Yeah, well, that's if she ever lets me claim her. She's still convinced Mitchell is her one and only. I made the stupid suggestion of using me as jealousy bait so she thinks everything I do is part of this plan to get the stupid dog."

"So tell her how you feel."

"And scare her off? I can't take the chance. Nor can I interfere with her plan to capture Mitchell's interest for fear she'll hate me."

More laughter filled his ear. "Ahh, poor baby brother. I'd wager that you're slated to be in a threesome like me and Ethan. Can you handle sharing?"

"Never thought about it," he answered honestly. "Then again, I also never thought I'd ever find a mate like you either. The idea of having to share her with another man…" Should have disgusted him, made him walk away, done something other than rouse his curiosity as to how he'd feel watching her in the arms of another. Or more decadent, joining in.

He'd seen the happiness Ethan and his brother shared with Naomi, heard their indiscreet cries of pleasure as they spent every night together, the three of them at once. Could he handle it? *If it means pleasing Francine? Probably, dammit.*

"Don't let the whole other guy thing wig you out. Just keep your focus on her and you'll see the pleasure is well worth it. But discussing my sex life wasn't the reason why I called. Some dude has been staking out the neighborhood and I think it's because of you."

"Oh that's priceless. Blame me even if I'm not there."

"Who else should I blame when the truck we found stashed in the woods has plates with a dealership sticker from our hometown?"

A curse slipped from him. "What does the stalker look like?"

As Javier described the man, Alejandro's grip on the phone tightened to the point he heard plastic cracking. "Fuck. He followed me."

"Who?"

"Bloody hunter whose daughter I banged one night drunk. I think he saw me shifting in the woods when I left her room."

"You fucking idiot."

"It wasn't my fault. I'd left her bedroom and thought I was alone. The bastard was hiding in a blind wearing some fucking animal piss that masked his scent. He took a pot shot at me, but I got away.

The next day, I heard he was in town making inquiries, trying to find out who I was. Rather than lead him to Mama and the others, I thought I'd take a vacation and visit family."

"And led him straight to us."

"I'm sorry. I didn't expect him to find my trail." A trite reply to a possible sticky situation.

Javier sighed. "Don't worry about it. Shit happens. I'll let the neighborhood know and we'll be on our guard. You might want to stay away from here though. I don't want Naomi in danger."

Just the thought of her or the babies she carried getting hurt made him sick to his stomach. "I should probably go to a hotel so that Francine is safe too."

"And leave her alone if he's already found you?"

Double fuck. He couldn't leave her unguarded. "Good point. Thanks for the warning. I'll keep my eyes peeled."

They exchanged good-byes and hung up. Staring at the ceiling where the sound of water running had stopped, he couldn't help clenching his fists in anger. *If that bastard dares to harm a hair on her head…* He'd kill him, pure and simple.

Chapter Seven

Hanging off his arm, nattering nonstop, Mitchell refrained from sighing at Jenny's annoying presence. In the past, he'd never noticed certain things about her, such as her too slim frame—unlike someone's plush, curvy one. Ignored her habit of using too much makeup—so different from a certain fresh-faced girl with freckles he knew. Tuned out her stupid attempts at conversation, while recalling the fun he'd had verbally sparring with another.

Even on a date with a girl guaranteed to give him a good time, he couldn't stop thinking about Francine. Worst, he kept comparing her to Jenny, and poor Jenny, she couldn't seem to win in any category.

He'd actually begun thinking of ways to ditch his eager date when *they* came in. Looking ridiculously gorgeous—and nothing like a sister, dammit—Francine wore a short red skirt that flared, a tight top that showed off cleavage deep enough to swallow a hand, oh and a certain cat, whose possessive arm around her staked his claim quite effectively.

Bright eyes only lightly outlined with dark eyeliner skimmed over him, and he didn't miss the quirk of her lips as she took in his date who chose that moment to hang herself on his neck like a pendant. Before he could disentangle her, Francine tugged at Alejandro, leading him toward the bar, but Alejandro changed her direction, instead leading her onto the dance floor.

It briefly crossed Mitchell's mind to wonder what she did here, this techno club not her usual hang out. His sister and Francine usually preferred cocktail type bars. Not that how she'd gotten here mattered. Present, and looking entirely too delicious, he couldn't push her from his mind. An irrational urge came over him. He needed to see her, touch her. *Mark her,* whispered his wolf. However, instead of doing any of those things, he stayed put, and lost sight of her among the dense bodies. His beast just about lost its mind, pacing and growling that he find her. Surely a peek wouldn't hurt, a glimpse to ensure nothing untoward happened whilst in the grips of the seducer.

"Let's dance." He dragged Jenny, craning to locate a mop of auburn curls, and when he found it, both man and beast let out a low growl. Stopping dead on the dance floor, he watched as Francine danced with Alejandro, her hourglass shape undulating to the music's fast tempo, the cat's hands on her hips guiding her. A hypnotic sight if he ignored the other male and imagined himself in his stead.

An arm wrapped around him from behind, a bony frame pressing up to his back. Jenny shouted in his ear, "I thought we were going to dance?"

Pivoting, he tried not to let his annoyance show on his face. Poor Jenny. She'd done nothing to deserve his ire. He moved jerkily to the toe-tapping rhythm, trying not to cringe when his date kept rubbing against him. Harder to fight was his urge to peer back at Francine and see what she did. He lost that battle. Twirling Jenny, he swapped places with her in time to catch the girl that he could no longer consider as a sister, dirty dancing with the cat. Facing away from Alejandro, she gyrated her buttocks against him while the seducer let his hands roam over her stomach, sliding them to a point just under her breasts then down again to clasp her hips.

Unbidden, Mitchell's cock swelled at the sight, their dance so mesmerizing and sensual that he wanted to join them, press in on her from the front, have her hands wander over his back as he hungrily devoured her mouth.

"Mitchell," yelled a voice that didn't sound like a husky promise coated in laughter. "I'm so flattered." It took a hand cupping his crotch for him to clue in on what Jenny meant. He recoiled from her touch, repulsed and imbued with a sense of guilt. Not at having gotten caught lusting for another woman, but because he didn't want Francine to see Jenny touching him.

His distaste didn't go unnoticed. Confusion twisted Jenny's face, and he could see her opening her mouth to speak. An answer eluded him so he took the cowardly route. He turned on his heel and made a beeline for the bar.

Unfortunately, she followed, not so easily ditched.

"What the fuck is wrong with you?" Jenny asked, her fingers digging into his arm, trying to stop him.

"This was a bad idea." Such a bad idea, because like a fever, thoughts of Francine consumed him, and his Jenny remedy just wouldn't do.

"What was a bad idea? Dancing? We can leave anytime you like. My roommate's gone for the night. We've got the place to ourselves," she said seductively, pressing herself to his side.

God, how he wished he could take her up on the offer. Screw something until this crazy mess in his head sorted itself. But the thought of banging Jenny and not Francine shriveled his dick better than an arctic swim.

Shit, how to get out of this pickle? Honesty seemed like his best option. Wasn't that what women always clamored for? "The mistake I meant was you and me going on a date. I'm sorry, Jenny, you're a nice girl and all, but I think we need to just be friends."

Her jaw dropped and hurt made her eyes glisten. "But, I thought you wanted to be with me? Isn't that why you called? I mean, everyone knows you and me are going to get together eventually. You just need to sow some oats first before you settle down."

Feeling like an ass, but needing to make sure she didn't misunderstand, Mitchell took a deep breath before speaking. "Listen, Jenny. I called you because I was horny. It was wrong of me, I admit it. But I realize now, I can't do that to you. It wouldn't be fair."

"How is it unfair if I'm willing? You don't have to propose to me tonight. Let's just go back to my place and I'll show you why you made the right call."

She clutched at him, and Mitchell pried her fingers free, trying to refrain from grimacing in distaste. "No. I can't. I was trying to use you to forget someone else, but it's not going to work. We aren't going to work. I'm sorry. I'll just drive you home."

"Who is she?"

"No one." *The hottest woman alive.* "I'm sorry, Jenny. Come on, I'll give you a ride."

Anger twisted Jenny's features. "Screw you, Mitchell. Don't do me any fucking favors. I'll get my own ass home, and it won't be alone," she yelled, shoving at his chest before stalking away.

Sighing, he turned back to the bar and ordered a beer. Despite the nastiness of the past moment, relief swept through him, quickly followed by urgency, make that an overwhelming need to keep tabs on Francine. Sweating brown bottle in hand, he sauntered over to the edge of the dance floor, calling himself all kinds of stupid for doing it, but unable to stay away. Sipping his brew, he found himself riveted by the sight of Francine dancing in the arms of her lover. *Or is it mate like she implied?* Even the thought roused his wolf, which paced in his mind with a snarl. A rumbling sound of discontent slipped from him that increased with each beer he downed, watching as the girl he lusted after, pure and simple, enjoyed herself in the arms of another.

When Alejandro finally left her side, making his way to the men's room, Mitchell weaved a path to her side where she stood sipping some fluorescent tinted drink.

"Are you and he an item?" His question emerged terse and abrupt.

Brown eyes of the sweetest chocolate perused him. Her lips pursed, their fullness captivating him. "Would you care if we were? Or are you going to feed me that bullshit about me being a sister and all again?"

"I was just trying to look out after you. I care about you, Francine." *And I want to kiss you, dammit.*

"But you don't love me," she stated baldly.

The answer she wanted eluded him. Did he love her? Yes, but as a lover? He wanted her, with an erotic urgency that surprised him. But, he couldn't lie and tell her he loved her when he still saw her as little more than a friend—a hot and sexy one. "No. But—"

"Do you love Jenny?"

"No. Of course not."

A heavy sigh left her. "What do you want from me, Mitchell? You want to fuck? Is that it?"

"Yes. No." He scrubbed hand through his hair, frustrated but still unsure of what he wanted. Actually, he knew what he wanted. To strip her naked, lick every inch of her, then fuck her with his cock until she screamed in his arms. But, at the same time, doing that would open a huge can of worms that he didn't think he was prepared for. "I want things to go back the way they were, when it wasn't so freakn' complicated."

"You mean before I forced you to actually pay attention to me. To realize I am a woman with needs. A woman looking for her mate to claim her, or at least put out the fire in her body."

97

"A part of me wants to," he whispered, reaching a hand out to stroke a tendril of hair from her face. "But another part of me keeps screaming it's wrong."

"I'm not going to wait forever."

"Can't you wait long enough for me to sort through this mess in my head? I don't want to rush into something that we'll both regret."

Disappointment flashed in her eyes, and before she could answer, the cat returned, his arm sliding around her from behind. Jealousy stung Mitchell at the casual way she accepted Alejandro's embrace and the easy way she leaned back into his body, finding refuge in his touch. *I should be the one holding her!*

"We were talking," he growled.

The seducer fixed him with a cold stare. "No, you were making excuses. Again. And I'm tired of it. Some of us aren't afraid to admit our feelings. To act." Brazenly, Alejandro, ran a hand up her torso until he cupped a breast. Francine's breathing hitched, but she did nothing to remove his palm, and an urge to cup her other breast came over Mitchell. He almost had to grab his hand to stop it from actually doing it.

He took a step back in the hopes some space would help him regain control. The cat's words penetrated. "You're mates?"

"Not yet, but we will be," Alejandro said with calm assurance. But Mitchell didn't miss the surprise in Francine's eyes when he said it.

"Don't do it, Francine," he said, his jealousy winning the battle. "He's a womanizer. He'll fuck you then leave you for the first pussy that comes his way. He'll make you—"

Faster than he would have credited the bastard, Alejandro tucked Francine behind him and threw the first punch, the force of it making Mitchell stagger, his ears ringing. With a roar of rage, and using his turmoil—and blue balls—to fuel it, he attacked back. Fists swinging, he fought the bastard who thought to claim Francine. Who thought to touch the silky skin that he dreamt of. Who kissed the lips that should press against his. Who dared to try and claim his woman.

The screams of bystanders along with the cheers faded away into the background as he slugged it out with Alejandro, the satisfying sound of his fist connecting with flesh making him grin savagely. A smile lost when a right hook back loosened some teeth.

The fight only lasted minutes before the bouncers, shapeshifters on steroids who almost rivaled Ethan in size, pried them apart and tossed their asses out of the club. Sprawled on the pavement, Mitchell raised his head, his beast pulsing at the forefront. He snarled, baring his teeth. The damned cat, on all fours, tossed his head back and growled right back, his eyes more animal than human. Their staring match ended up broken by a curvy pair of calves. Letting his gaze travel up the skin, Mitchell swallowed as he saw right up Francine's short skirt. He couldn't help but stare at the damp fabric clinging to a cleft whose scent drifted down to him like the sweetest of perfumes.

"Are you done?" she demanded, tapping a foot. "And you can stop looking up my skirt, Mitchell. I am not happy with either of you. I am not some fucking toy that you can use in your testosterone match of tug of war."

"I'm sorry, Francine." The cat's immediate reply came out contrite, and Mitchell sneered.

"Pussy."

"Enough," she yelled. "Did you not just hear me, Mitchell? For a guy who can't say the words 'I want you', you're acting like a possessive jerk."

"Fine. I want you," he bit out with a triumphant look at the cat.

"Bullshit. You only think you do because Alejandro had the balls to say he did first. What if he left right now? Would you still say that?"

Would he? If the cat were gone tomorrow, and he didn't have to worry about Francine in the arms of another, could he go back to his life the way it was? Turmoil free?

"Time's up. Wrong answer."

"But, I didn't say anything," he protested.

"Exactly," she said. "I'm done. Alejandro, take me home."

Turning, she stalked toward the parking lot, and the cat shot him an exultant smile before springing to his feet and following. A red film descended over his eyes, and Mitchell jumped to his feet, ready to charge the bastard again when Jenny, in a blonde fury, stepped in front of him.

"She's what you ditched me for?" she screeched. "That tubby orphan Annie wannabe? You've got to be fucking kidding me. I am a hundred times better than that slut. That…"

Mitchell tuned Jenny out as he watched Alejandro open Francine's car door to seat her then slide into the driver's seat. He ignored her until the red taillights winked out of view, then came back to himself and actually heard the invectives Jenny kept hurling about Francine.

"Shut the fuck up, you anorexic slut," he snapped. His rebuke made her recoil, but it did nothing to wipe the rage from her twisted features.

"I will not. Since when do you want that redheaded cow?"

"I don't want her," he answered automatically.

"Oh, please. Everyone in the club could see you watching her, staring at her like you wanted to eat her up." Jenny sneered. "But the great part is it looks to me like she doesn't want you."

"You don't know what the hell you're talking about. It's complicated. And none of your damned business."

She spat at him. "Fuck you, Mitchell. I can do better than you."

Off she stalked, leaving Mitchell alone finally, and it was then he realized the answer he should have given Francine. *Yes, I want you.* Worst, he should have probably admitted that to her, and himself, years ago. But he'd waited too long and now the woman who tied him in knots left with another. *And I've lost my chance.*

* * * *

"Are you okay?" Alejandro's soft question snapped her from her vacant stare out the car window.

"No. I'm now wondering if I should have said or done something different with Mitchell. But, I got so mad when instead of admitting he felt something for me, he pretended the whole asshole act was to protect me."

"It's not easy to admit you care about somebody."

A bitter laugh slipped from her. "So I'm noticing. I think I'm going to forget our plan to make him jealous. It's worked too well. The only problem is while he's jealous, he still doesn't want to do anything about it. Make that, he wants nothing to do with me."

"Mitchell's an idiot. So forget the dog. Let's make the act reality."

Puzzled, she turned to look at him. "What are you trying to say? You want to keep pretending we're a couple?"

"Not all of us were faking it," he said in a wry tone.

"I don't understand."

Stopped at a red light, Alejandro banged his head off the steering wheel. "God, for a smart woman, you are so freakn' clueless sometimes. I'm saying I'm not faking it, baby. I feel things for you. Intense things."

"You're horny. I get that. So am I. If you want to fuck, just say so. I could use a bit of stress relief."

A groan escaped him. "You talk about Mitchell being dense. I. Want. You. Not just your body, all of you, dammit."

Surprise made her gape at him. "You do?"

"Why do you sound so shocked? Did you really think the whole thing was an act? Mitchell was only our audience for little bits. And I wasn't exactly subtle."

"I thought that was what you did with all the ladies. You know, flirting being akin to breathing for you."

"I am a flirt. I don't deny that. But I don't make women dinner, or breakfast. I smile. We fuck. I leave."

"Ooh, now that sounds fun. So once we fuck," she repeated crudely, "you'll leave."

"No. I'm not going anywhere, baby. It's not the same with you."

"And why would I believe that?"

"Because everything about you is different." They pulled into her driveway, and he turned to her, tugging at her hands until he held them clasped in his warm ones. "It might have started out as a ruse, but the more time we spend together, the more I want to be with you. And not just naked. I want to cook for you and hear that delightful noise you make when you eat something you like. I want you tease me mercilessly and make raunchy innuendos. Waking up beside you, picking you up from work, dancing cheek to cheek, running through the woods. All things I want to share with you, and only you."

Blinking seemed about the only thing she could do while he spoke. Heck, she couldn't even breathe while he said the words she'd waited so long to hear someone say. It no longer mattered that it turned out Mitchell wouldn't say them first or at all. Alejandro, man and cat, drove her wild, and not just with lust. Funny thing was, she wanted to discover all those things about him too, plus some. But could she trust him with her heart? Despite what Naomi, and even he said, could she believe that he'd find contentment with her, and only her? Could she afford to not try?

"That's a long list. Are we going to have time for screwing? Because I really like to screw. Oh, and suck cock. And—"

He placed his hand over her mouth. "Enough, you evil brat. I swear you're trying to make my balls explode."

She mumbled something against his hand. He took it away. "What did you say?"

"No, but I'd like to make your cock explode." His strangled moan made her giggle. "Okay, I'll admit it. I want your furry ass too, and not just for a spin atop your cock. You intrigue me. But, I have to say, letting you get close scares me too." She decided to speak with him honestly.

"You're afraid of losing Mitchell."

"No. I'm afraid of losing you. My biggest fear is after a few days or a week, you'll tire of me and move on. I don't know if I could handle that, Alejandro." Heck, she'd lacked the ability to make her own parents stick around, and they were supposed to love her. How could she manage to intrigue a man like Alejandro for a life time?

"If I make a promise to you, I will keep it. If say forever, it will be for an eternity."

How I want to believe. She reached up a hand and placed it on his cheek. "Can we start with just tonight?"

"So you don't want me to mark you?" He seemed saddened by it.

"Not yet. I've known you what now, thirty-six hours? That's pretty quick to make a decision that lasts a lifetime."

"It happened to my brother and Ethan."

"And yet it still took them a week to convince Naomi. Don't I deserve the same? I promise to not try and rip your balls off like she tried with Javier."

"Ah, but I'd love for you to get rough with them," he said with a leer and a chuckle.

"Pig." It came out as a term of endearment, and finally, he leaned forward to touch his mouth to hers. It started out as a slow, sensual kiss, but Francine wanted, make that needed, more.

She curled her arms around his neck and yanked him tight to her, grinding her mouth against his, sucking his lower lip before biting it, not hard enough to break skin, but with enough pressure to excite them both.

The horn honked and they sprang apart, him with a curse, her with a giggle.

"Shall me adjourn somewhere more comfortable?" he asked.

"Think we can make it to a bed?" she challenged, hopping out of the car. In a flash, he'd come around to her side and swooped her into his arms.

"A bed? Where's your sense of spirit?" he chided as he juggled her and the keys up her front walk. She latched onto his neck, sucking the tanned skin, loving the slightly salty flavor and inhaling his rich scent. Her antics caused the usually graceful cat to fumble, the keys clinking against the lock. He growled, his impatience clear—and so arousing.

Chuckling against his skin, she let her hand travel the breadth of his upper chest, stroking him while he fitted the key into the lock and managed to get the door open.

Kicking it closed, the door swung back, not entirely latching shut, not that she cared given he'd let her slide down the length of his hard frame. She kept her arms wound around his neck, stretching on tiptoe to reach his lips. Bending, he gave her his mouth, the passion of their embrace stealing her breath.

"I want you, Jag," she moaned against his lips. "Hurry."

"Impatient brat," he murmured against her mouth as his hands pulled up her top and slid over the skin of her back. Returning the favor, she tugged at his shirt, but pressed tightly together, they made little progress. They split apart long enough to tear them off, leaving her clad in a bra and him bare-chested.

Good lord, talk about scrumptious. She reverently ran her fingers over the taut, tanned skin of his torso, loving the way he sucked in his breath as her hands slid over the ripples of his abs following the vee of ridged flesh that disappeared into his jeans.

She unsnapped his pants and tugged them down over his hips, dropping to her knees as she did. Eye level with his cock, she licked her lips in impatience as she struggled to denude him.

"What are you doing?" he growled.

"I am going to suck that big cock of yours just like I've wanted to since I saw you shafting it last night."

"Oh fuck me, you're trying to kill me," he moaned as she freed his long and curved prick. The velvety skin fairly scorched her palm as she wrapped her hand around it, the veins in it pulsing at her touch. Peering up, she saw him gazing down at her, his dark eyes blazing with passion. Holding his stare, she stuck her tongue out and lapped at his rounded head, tasting the pre-cum on the tip before swirling it down the ridge that ran the length of it. He swallowed hard, the cords on his neck standing out as she lapped at him, learning every inch of his cock before she took him into her mouth in one wet gulp.

"Oh god, baby, that feels so freakn' good," he groaned as his fingers tangled themselves in her hair, his grip on her head exciting, especially when he helped her bob his dick in and out of her wet orifice.

Pulsing in her mouth, his prick gliding in and out, she inhaled hard, wanting to see him lose control.

"Fuck. Fuck. Fuck." He panted the word like a mantra, his body taut as he held back from giving her what she wanted.

She mewled in disappointment when he pulled her off of his cock. He lifted her right off her feet and caught her lips in a fiery kiss that stole her breath. As he slammed her up against a wall, she welcomed his savage need, his loss of control for her. His hands tore at the closure for her skirt. With a curse, he ripped the waistband and pushed it down over her hips. The loose material slid down her legs and she stepped out of them, never losing her contact with his lips. Big hands cupped her almost nude cheeks, squeezing them even as he yanked her against him, grinding himself, all hot and hard, against her lower stomach.

"Stop playing," she growled. "And fuck me."

"As my lady commands." Hoisting her up by the cheeks, automatically her legs wrapped around his waist, her damp panties pressing against his lower stomach while his shaft nudged against the crease of her ass. He pressed her back against the wall to brace her as one of his hands slid under her, rubbing against the moist fabric.

"So wet, baby," he whispered. "Wet for me. Do you want me? Do you want this?"

The hard length of his cock see-sawed across her covered cleft and she whimpered, lust stealing her ability to speak actual words.

Ripping fabric barely registered over the sound of their panting, but she noticed immediately the scorching difference when he rubbed himself against her, the silken skin of his dick slick with her juices.

"Fuck me," she begged.

"Until you come hard and scream," he promised then he slammed his cock home. A yell emerged from her, a savage cry of satisfaction as he pumped her, his curved length filling her up. Clenching tight around him, she plastered him with passionate kisses, sucking his tongue into her mouth and swallowing his groans of pleasure.

Inside her head, her wolf spun, making demands that Francine wasn't ready for yet. Ordering her to claim this man. It revived her enough to say in a breathless voice, "No marking." Even if all she wanted to do was bite him all over and show the world he belonged to her.

"Not tonight. But you will be mine," he growled, pistoning her faster. Gripping her ass cheeks, he thrust even harder into her, the rough friction making her squeeze tight as her pleasure coiled tighter and tighter.

Something, a sound that didn't involve fucking, a smell out of place, made her open her eyes, eyes blurred with passion. Framed in her doorway stood Mitchell and he watched their frantic coupling with feverish eyes. He caught her staring at him, but instead of leaving or interrupting, he cupped himself, squeezing his hard bulge.

It proved too much. Her head went back and she screamed as her orgasm swept her over the edge. And still Alejandro pumped her, his slick prick slamming home, again and again, triggering a second orgasm that made her body arch in a taut bow, so intensely did it race through her. Her channel spasmed tight around him and he yelled as he came, his cream spurting into her hotly.

Spent, she could only lie in his arms limply, their harsh breathing mixing. When he shifted to improve his grip and carry her upstairs, she peered at her front door and saw it closed. Mitchell gone. *Or never here to begin with.* But she didn't have time to analyze reality from imagination as Alejandro began kissing her again, murmuring, "My sweet Francine."

The awe and affection in his voice humbled her. But not as much as the fact his semi-hard cock still buried inside her began to thicken again. A man with stamina. How perfect because Francine was far from done with her big cat. *And if this is to be our only time together, I better make it count.* Because despite his pretty words, she still couldn't quite believe he wouldn't leave and move on to greener pastures.

* * * *

Mitchell panted, his head bowed over the steering column of his car. Inside his pants, his cock throbbed, aching and ready to forget his misgivings and take what Francine had offered him for so long. What he'd now lost in his stubborn refusal to recognize the prize before his very eyes. The woman who made no bones that she wanted him, and when rejected, turned to another.

He'd not meant to walk in on their lovemaking. Although, a part of him had known what he'd see when he'd approached her partially ajar front door, the soft sounds of her moans and the fleshy slap of bodies fucking too blatant for him to not decipher. It didn't stop him from entering. Coming across her, pinned against the wall, her legs wrapped around Alejandro's flanks, his taut buttocks pumping while she clung to him, her fingers digging into his skin, should have sent him into a rage. Embarrassed him at the very least. Instead, it made him rock hard. Unable to tear himself away, he'd watched as the cat gave the woman he couldn't erase anymore from his mind what he didn't dare. Alejandro made love to her, fucked her with sensual intensity, and she enjoyed every hard thrust of it.

When she'd opened her eyes and seen him, her lids heavy with passion, he'd expected her to yell at him to get out or to tell Alejandro. She did neither. Instead, she held his gaze, the invitation to join them so damned clear. He almost did. His hand even reached down to cup himself, stroke his turgid member through his pants. As if the sight of his excitement were too much, she'd come with a long scream that made his balls tighten and almost shoot their load.

In those seconds, he'd almost forgotten his aversion to the cat, his trepidation over being with his sister's best friend, and even the fear of the commitment she offered. For more than a fleeting moment, he wanted, with an intensity that shocked him, to belong to her, whether as part of a threesome or not. He could even so easily imagine taking turns with the seducer, pleasuring her lusty body, muffling her cries with his cock as Alejandro took her from behind. Erotic images that stunned him and sent him fleeing.

Not ready. Frightened.

His emotions swirled inside him, a cacophony of sensations that made him sit in his car, unable to move while he fought to regain control. It didn't help that his wolf nipped at the edges of his mind, demanding to know why they didn't go back to mark the female, to stake their claim.

But mating with Francine had taken on a whole new dimension. Claiming her also meant accepting the cat. It meant sharing a woman, a home, possibly even a bed. Could he handle that? Probably not given each time he saw the bastard, he wanted to wipe the smug look off his face with his fist.

He needed advice, but who could he turn to? His mother, who'd clawed the face of the last female bitch who'd thought to grab her mate's ass? His brothers, whose solution would probably rhyme with beat the crap out of? He did know one person, make that two actually, who would possibly understand what he went through. Who could maybe explain how they managed to share without turning his sister's house into a war zone. But given the late hour, it would have to wait until morning.

Amped up on emotion, and hornier than a fucking bunny in heat, Mitchell made it home, but sat in his car instead of going inside. Indoors, he'd just wander restlessly or toss and turn. If he woke his mother, she'd pry the uncomfortable truth from him, or cuff him upside the head. Neither scenario appealed.

The serenity of the forest called him along with the mindless peace he knew he'd find in letting his beast free for a run. Stripping, he placed his clothes on the passenger seat of his car and got out. Naked, he stretched, enjoying the cool night air on his body. Then clenching his teeth, he shifted, letting the animal mind that resided within him bound forth and take control.

As his wolf emerged, which involved a painful cracking and re-shaping of limbs, his senses grew even sharper. The myriad scents of the outside filtered themselves into identifiable things like grass, rubber, a wandering coon…and a female bear?

Cocking his head, he sniffed, sucking in a deep lungful, trying to figure out why the scent appeared so odd. He could tell right off that the scent didn't belong to a shapeshifter, the human overtone that melded with a shifter's animal odor a distinctive marker. And yet, he knew for a fact no bears roamed these parts. No large predators did given they'd claimed the forested tract behind the strip of houses as shapeshifter land. Natural creatures smartly stayed away, or had in the past, which made the odd-smelling bear's presence beyond strange.

Putting his nose to the ground, Mitchell followed the trail, growing more baffled as it led to the base of a tree across from his sister's house. Sure, bears climbed them, but not big sows, and not without leaving marks. The bark didn't show any of the deep gouges from claws he'd expect to see. A glimpse up showed him nothing but shadows.

Circling the base of the large oak, sniffing to see if he'd tracked wrong, he froze as he heard a whisper of sound from above him. Peering up, he dove sideways as he caught a glint of metal. *Bang!*

The shot grazed past his shoulder, taking hair and a sliver of skin with it, the gouge burning like hell. Fuck. Not a bear, but something worse. A hunter.

Snarling, and unable to shift because the human might see, Mitchell began to howl in warning, knowing either his brother's or Naomi's mates would come running. Lights flicked on and as doors opened. A second shot went whizzing past, burying itself in the dirt in front of his paw. Mitchell darted sideways, barking to draw help to him, not stupid enough to think he was a match for a gun shot at close range by an asshole in a tree. A third shot buried itself in his side, and he yipped at the fiery pain, almost missing the sound of feet hitting the ground. Agony or not, he whipped around with a snarl in time to see a shadow running away. He limped after the hunter, but the pain proved excruciating, if inexplicable. He'd suffered worse before.

As he slumped to the ground, he heard the sound of animals baying and running footsteps. Then, the more disturbing sound of an engine starting and tires spinning.

But he found it hard to care that his prey escaped as he passed out.

Chapter Eight

A feathery touch tickled down Francine's spine, and she squirmed to make it stop. It lightly stroked her again, and she grunted as she rolled onto her back to stop it. A warm hand landed on her bare breast, cupping it, and she froze, her next breath halted. *Oh my God, he's still here.* The realization both warmed her and sent a chill of fear through her because she didn't know what to do.

She'd not exactly expected Alejandro to disappear like Houdini before she woke, but she'd never expected to wake up beside him. While she'd had boyfriends in the past, short term ones, she'd never had one spend the night. At a loss as to what she should do, she kept her eyes clamped tight and tried to breathe shallowly lest he discover her less than pleasant morning breath.

"You're not very good at faking sleep," Alejandro said wryly, squeezing her breast before rolling her nipple between his fingers.

With a gasp, her eyes flew open, and she saw him propped on one elbow staring down at her while his other hand continued to palpate her breast.

"Um, hi. I didn't expect to see you."

A frown tightened his lips. "I told you I wouldn't leave."

At his disgruntled tone, she hurried to explain. "That came out wrong. It's not that I expected you to run off at the crack of dawn, it's just," she lowered her voice to a whisper, "no one's ever spent the whole night with me before." A blush heated its way up her cheeks as she admitted it.

"Probably because you steal the blankets and hate to cuddle," he retorted, diluting his rebuke with a smile and squeeze of her boob.

"I like to cuddle. Well, I do when I'm awake anyway."

"I'll test that claim later, but I can tell you right now when you sleep, it's on your stomach, clutching your pillow, and every time I touched you, you elbowed me. At one point, you even kicked me."

She could only grin sheepishly. "Oops. Sorry, I guess I'm not used to sharing."

"Well, get used to it, baby, because while I don't have much experience sleeping with someone either, I'd like to start doing it with you. But…" He released her breast to wag a finger at her. "I also don't want to wake up freezing on a sliver of mattress, looking for something to hold on to for fear of falling on the floor."

"Whiner."

"Brat."

They grinned at each other and laughed. He dropped a kiss on her nose, but she cringed anyway. "Toothbrush first."

"I've already brushed," he admitted. "I'll go make breakfast while you take care of yourself. You need to get ready for work, and since I'm going to be sticking around, I need to start looking for a job."

"Really? You're serious about staying even though I wouldn't let you claim me?"

He flicked her nipple and she yelped. "You are really asking for a spanking. I meant what I said and as far as I'm concerned, I claimed you all right, baby. It might have only been your body last night, but I'm pretty sure I've already got my hooks in your heart, which just means I need to win your trust. And that starts with me putting down some roots."

Biting her lip, she fought not to throw herself on him and kiss him silly. She'd probably kill him with her morning dragon breath if she did. But once she did wash herself up, he was in for a big smackeroo. And if she had time before work, a BJ too. "Sounds good. Now get that sweet ass of yours moving. I thought I heard the mention of breakfast and after last night's workout, I am starved." She winked and he groaned.

"Gonna kill me for sure. Wasn't three times enough, baby? A man's only got so much stamina."

She grinned. "Buy some vitamins if you can't keep up. I'm a lusty girl. Get used to it."

"My pleasure." He gave her nipple one last tweak before rolling off the bed and strutting off in nothing but skin, glorious tanned skin that felt so freakn' good against hers.

Humming to herself, she showered and brushed her teeth, getting ready for work in record time, still determined to indulge in a morning quickie before she had to leave. Skipping down the stairs, she grinned at the smell of bacon. *I could get used to this. Used to him.* He'd brought her to heaven last night, more than once, and she'd never felt better or happier. She never wanted the pleasurable glow he'd given her last night to fade.

Entering the kitchen, she found her sexy cat flipping French toast in a frying pan, still naked.

"Aren't you afraid of burning some important parts?" she asked, munching on a strip of bacon while watching him move, hunger of a different sort making her body warm.

Hooded eyes met hers. "Don't worry, baby. I won't let anything harm me and get in the way of your pleasure."

Laughter bubbled from her as she went around to the sink to wash her hands of the grease. Arms bracketed her, and she turned to find Alejandro's face hovering only an inch away. "Morning. Can I get a kiss now?"

She pretended to think about it, and laughed as his hands bracketed her waist and pulled her to him. "Brat." He crushed his mouth to hers, and she sighed against him as, that easily, her arousal came roaring back to enflame her.

Lifting her, he seated her on the lip of the sink, and she wrapped her legs around his waist as she sucked his tongue into her mouth, enjoying his low growl of pleasure.

"I'm going to burn your breakfast," he murmured into her mouth before sliding his lips down to nibble at her jawline.

"I'm sure I could find something else to eat," she quipped, threading her fingers into his hair and yanking him back up to kiss her again. Things got pretty hot after that with their lips fused and her hips gyrating as she dry humped his hard cock, now cursing herself for dressing before she came down.

Glass shattered and she vaguely wondered what they'd broken in their impromptu romp just as a sharp sting in her back made her cry out.

"Francine!" Alejandro's frantic yell came through white noise that roared in her ears. She tried to gather herself to answer, but found herself coughing instead, fluid bubbling at her lips. The world tilted as he pulled her down below the level of the counter, repeating the word "shit" over and over.

"Where's the fucking phone?" he growled as he cradled her in his arms, his tone panicked.

"Wall," she muttered, the word emerging out as sluggish sounding as she felt. "What happened? I feel funny. Kind of cold and numb." She had to force each syllable past a tongue gone thick, and she blinked as her vision blurred.

"Someone shot you," he said, his voice low and tight. If she didn't know better, she would have said her affable cat was pissed—and scared. She found it hard to concentrate on anything with the ice spreading through her body. He laid her down gently on her stomach, and she almost welcomed the cold tile floor on her cheek because at least she could feel it.

Alejandro scooted to the wall to grab the phone. He yanked it down and scurried back to her while punching in numbers furiously. Her eyelids fluttered shut. A tap on her cheek made her open them.

"Stay with me, baby. I'm going to get you some help. Answer the fucking phone," he yelled when whomever he called didn't immediately pick up. "Javier, about fucking time you answered. He shot her. What do you mean who? Francine, you idiot. In the fucking back. I need help. Now! I think he used silver."

Silver? Well that sucked. Who wanted her dead? Shapeshifters could heal from a lot of things, but silver interfered with that ability. *And that's not good.* Because she now knew the spreading numbness meant she'd gotten hit bad.

She wanted to tell Alejandro, whose face hovered over hers fixed in a mask of devastation, that everything would be okay, but her lashes fluttered as darkness sucked her down.

* * * *

Helplessness. What an awful feeling, and one Alejandro never experienced before. It bothered him as much as the fear that gripped him when he thought of Francine not recovering. *No! She has to get better. I won't let her die.*

Alejandro paced in front of the door that hid him from Francine and the doctor they'd called to take care of her. The ride to Naomi's house with Francine pale and unconscious would haunt him forever. He'd not initially wanted to move her, but he feared even more her bleeding out from the silver embedded in her flesh, so he agreed to meet the physician at Naomi's house, which cut their travel time in half.

Borrowing Francine's car, he sped all the way, and said a prayer of thanks no cops stopped him on his way. Arriving in a squeal of tires at his brother's place, he almost cried in relief when he saw the doctor already there. Hands shaking, he feared moving the pale bundle in the back seat. Ethan pushed him aside and gently carried Francine inside, closeting her in the master bedroom for the physician to work on. The big Kodiak got shooed out by an ashen-faced Naomi who shook her head at Alejandro when he would have followed her inside.

"You're a mess, and besides, you need to tell everyone what's happened. She'll be okay, Alejandro. She has to be."

Hanging his head, moisture stinging his eyes, he prayed she spoke the truth.

"What the hell happened?" barked Geoffrey, Naomi's father, the grizzled wolf as angry as if his own daughter lay comatose.

Javier, Ethan and the rest of Naomi's family crowded around him, questioning looks in their eyes that turned to rage as he relayed the cowardly attack. It was when he heard about the hunter's potshots the night before, which still kept Mitchell abed this morn, that he lost his mind and roared.

"Why the fuck did no one call me?" If he'd known, he could have…still never expected such a brazen attack.

"It's my fault," Javier said. "I thought since he still staked out our house that he had no clue where you actually were."

"You thought wrong!" Alejandro growled and lunged at his brother, only to have Ethan hold him back.

121

"Punching him won't help things," rumbled the big Kodiak. "Dr. Weston is going to patch her up and she'll be fine. What we need to concentrate on is finding the hunter so he can't hurt anyone else. This has gone too far."

It had, and it was up to Alejandro to fix it. *I did this to her. And now I'll take care of it.* Because if there was one thing he would not tolerate, was someone hurting the woman he wanted as mate. *The woman I love.* The realization didn't come as too much of a surprise. He'd recognized how special she was from the moment they'd met. And after last night, only a forever after would satisfy him. He couldn't wait to tell her on bended knee how he felt. Once she recovered, that was.

Rarely did rage come to visit him, and never before for someone not related to him, but Francine meant more to him than anyone he'd ever known. He would have gladly stepped in front of her to take the bullet to spare her pain if given the chance. Anything to ease the ache inside at knowing she hurt. A pain in his heart that could only find ease in vengeance. But he wouldn't leave to wreak havoc until he knew she was safe.

It seemed like an eternity, but in reality was more like an hour before the doctor emerged, Naomi's mother at his side looking pale.

"She'll recover," the doctor announced, easing the fear inside him. "The bullet nicked her spine and lung. The hole in her lung has already sealed over, but the bone injury will take a little longer to heal. She's going to need quite a few days of bed rest. Oh, and lots of iron supplements, in other words, red meat to build up her blood because she lost quite a bit."

Relief made his breath whoosh out as the terror that had clung to him since he'd heard the shot finally loosened its grip. "Can I see her?"

"Go in, but not for long. She needs to rest. The silver made her weak and even though I've removed it, her body needs to regain its strength."

Leaving the gathered men, with the exception of Mitchell whom they'd tied to a bed in his own home so he could also recover, Alejandro entered the bedroom and approached the large bed with leaden feet. Sprawled on her stomach, covered in a blue sheet folded to her waist, the white bandage plastered to the middle of her back acted like a sucker punch to the gut. He staggered, and Naomi, her cheeks tear streaked, glanced at him and tried to give him a wan smile. He couldn't hold her gaze, the guilt making him look down where he saw her hand clutching Francine's tight.

Flipping her head the other way, Francine's weary brown eyes, so different from the passion-filled ones of the night before, peered up at him. It pierced him to see the happiness in her gaze when she saw him. How could she not blame him for her injury?

"Jag, thank god. Would you tell my BFF here that everything is all right? I swear, she's trying to crush my hand." Welcomed by his lover even though he didn't deserve it, Alejandro moved to stand behind Naomi.

"Oh stuff it," said Naomi in a thick voice still clogged with tears. "You didn't seem to mind when the doctor was digging that bullet out."

Turning back so she could see them both, Francine muttered, "Bitch."

"Skank." They both burst into giggles accompanied with watery eyes that they both surreptitiously wiped, Francine by rubbing her face against the pillow case.

"You're both fucked," he said, a ghost of a smile teasing his lips at their obviously long running joke.

"I sure was last night." Francine winked and licked her lips. "I don't know if the cow here was, although I bet once she's on her back, there's no getting her back up."

Instead of taking offence, Naomi laughed. "Javier likened me to a turtle, which believe me, he's paid for. His poor tongue is probably still sore from apologizing. But speaking of giant bovines, I'm going to send Ethan to fetch us a cow. The doctor said you needed to eat lots of red meat."

An inelegant snort came out of Francine. "Ha, nice try, pregnant one. You've just got a hankering for a big hunk of steak."

"Don't forget the baked potato and Caesar salad," Naomi added, rubbing her tummy with a smile.

"No wonder you're the size of a house."

"I am so getting a new best friend," Naomi grumbled.

"Good luck with that. No one else would put up with your snarky attitude."

"Love you, Francine," Naomi said in a wobbly voice as she stood up before slipping out the door.

"Love you too," Francine whispered, her voice tight.

Alejandro moved and took Naomi's vacated seat. He clasped Francine's just released hand. "Yours is a strange but beautiful friendship," he said, stroking his thumb over the pale skin of her hand.

"If you mean fucked up, then yeah. But it works for us. Thanks for getting me help."

He couldn't look her in eye, so guilty did he feel. "Don't thank me. It's my fault you got hurt in the first place."

"How do you figure that? The shot could have just as easily hit you."

"And the shooter probably meant to, given it's someone from my past who followed me here. I led them straight to you and now you're injured as a result."

"But you didn't know they'd do that."

"Doesn't matter. I'm still at fault."

"Damned fucking straight you are," Mitchell retorted from the doorway, bare-chested with a bandage wrapped around his shoulder and his arm in a sling. "Because you couldn't keep your dick in your pants, some fucking hunter is out there shooting at me and my family."

"You forgot me," Francine interjected.

Mitchell turned blazing eyes her way. "You are family, Francine. Sister or not, mate or not, no matter what you are, that won't ever fucking change. But him." Mitchell turned his attention back. "You've been nothing but trouble, sauntering into town like you own it. Seducing innocent girls—"

"One girl and the only one from here on in," Alejandro interjected.

"You seduced Francine! And now because of you, she's been shot. If I weren't wearing this fucking bandage—"

"And if you weren't terrified your mom would kill you," Francine interrupted with a snicker that earned her a glare.

"I should beat your furry ass right back to where it belongs," Mitchell snarled, stalking toward him.

"No need to exert yourself." Alejandro stood. "I need to leave anyway and take care of the situation. You're right. It is my fault, and I will fix it."

"No," Francine whispered. "Please don't go. I need you with me. Who will take care of me?" It sliced like a knife him to see her looking fearful, his beautiful brat who usually faced the world with a smile and a snappy comeback.

"You're in good hands here, and besides, do you really think Naomi's going to let you go anywhere?"

"But I don't want Naomi to hug me and tell me it's going to be all right."

His heart wrenched and if his honor didn't dictate he make her safe, he would have caved to her plea. As it was, he bent down and brushed his lips across hers. "I need to do this, baby. I need to make you safe. You won't be alone though. I have a feeling Mitchell won't leave your side. And isn't that what you've wanted all along?"

"But—"

"Shhh." He kissed her again, then stood to walk away. As he went to pass Mitchell, he grasped his good arm, and tugged him into the hall.

"Going to kiss me good-bye too, cat?" Naomi's brother mocked.

"You wish, dog. I just wanted to ask you to take care of her while I'm gone. I don't know how long it's going to take to hunt the bastard down, but I'm not going to be back until I know she's safe."

"Is this your way of bowing out and avoiding any scenes? How classy and predictable."

A snarl rose to Alejandro's lips and he shoved his forearm across Mitchell's throat, ramming him up against the wall. He kept his words low so Francine wouldn't hear him. "Listen here, and listen well. I care for Francine. Actually, that's an understatement. I am in love with her, and I want to claim her. Do you hear me, claim her as in forever. So don't think I'm not coming back, dog, because I am, and when I do, I will mark her. But because I love her, I'm asking you to watch over her while I'm gone. She needs someone to hold her and tell her it's going to be okay and despite the fact you're an idiot, she'd probably really like it if that person was you."

"You don't need to tell me what she needs. I have no intention of leaving her side, possibly ever again. So what are you going to do about that, cat? Still going to come back now knowing you're going to have competition? Or are you going to use this as your out so you can keep fucking your way across the country?"

Alejandro released him and stepped back, shaking his head with a light smile. "If you meant to scare me, try again. A threesome doesn't frighten me. Can you say the same though? I can't think of more fun than taking turns making love to her receptive body. The better question is, can you handle it? You'd better come up with an answer before I get back." Alejandro turned to leave, but he couldn't resist one parting shot. "Oh, and if you do decide to seduce her, she likes it when you bite down on her earlobe as you take her. Makes her go freakn' wild."

He chuckled as Mitchell's face turned red from embarrassment and desire. Hopefully, his hunt for the human who'd dared cross him wouldn't take long because Alejandro looked forward to the fireworks to come, both in and out of the bedroom.

* * * *

Returning to the bedroom, Mitchell seethed at the cat's words, but his anger receded in the face of Francine looking so small and helpless in the big bed. Of course, he should have known her tongue was in fine fighting shape.

"Are you guys done pissing on Naomi's walls? Or would you like to each grab one of my legs and pull me apart like a wishbone and see who gets the bigger piece?"

"You must be feeling better. You're trying to rip a strip off me," he remarked in a dry tone as he sat on the edge of the bed beside her. "Move over, you bed hog."

"No. I'm the injured one here."

"Excuse me? Do you think I'm wearing this bandage because it's fashionable?"

She peered over at him, her eyes lingering more on his nude torso than his bandage, which made him puff up his chest. "Wuss. My bandage is bigger than yours," she sassed, but she inched over a bit.

He slid down on the bed until he lay beside Francine, his head on the edge of the same pillow. Her eyes didn't meet his for long, focusing instead again on the white strips binding him. Then, as if unable to resist, her gaze strayed to the rest of his bare chest, heating him without a single touch. Mitchell grew hard under her regard, and cursed his loose track pants, which made that point all too evident. He tried to cover it with his hand but that just drew her attention to it.

"Nice wood. Hope you don't usually whack off with your left hand," she said with a snicker.

"You have a filthy mouth, Francine."

"All the better to do wicked things with. Hey, weren't you supposed to be tied to a bed somewhere to make sure you didn't get out and reopen your own gunshot wound?"

He shrugged. "They tried, but when I heard you got hurt, I kind of broke the bed to come see you." Which hurt like a fucking bitch, but he'd lost his freakn' mind when he heard about Francine's injury.

"Ah, isn't that the sweetest thing, but stop trying to distract me. What did you and Alejandro discuss?"

"He's leaving and told me to take care of you." He didn't bother lying.

"What? He wasn't serious, was he? He could get hurt."

Again, his shoulders lifted in dismissal while at the same time, irritation filled him that she seemed to care so much about the cat's wellbeing. *But obviously not enough to let him mark her last night.* Which meant he still had a chance. "Who cares? It's his fault we both got shot so it's only right he fix it."

"What is it with you guys and the macho bullshit about taking responsibility? Just because some psycho fixated on Jag doesn't mean it's his fault. Did he say how long he'll be gone?"

"He didn't. But, honestly, do you really think he's coming back?"

She bit her lip and didn't reply, but he saw the tears in her eyes. A twinge of guilt made him sigh and say, "I'm sure it will only be a day or so. Long enough to catch the human and stop him from hurting anyone else. But, you won't be alone. I'm not leaving your side."

"Gee, lucky me," she grumbled.

"What happened to we're meant to be together forever?" He said it in a teasing tone, but a part of him held his breath waiting for her reply, hoping he'd not completely fucked things up. Tied to a bed, with only his thoughts for company—his lonely state probably caused by him yelling at everyone to get out—left a man with way too much time to think. Hours to sift through his emotions and visualize one person over and over, and not just naked in his bed, but in his life, as a friend and lover.

He'd finally caught the damned mating fever and like a mask lifted from his eyes, he could now see Francine in a new light. See the merits in mating with someone who knew him and his family and didn't run in fear. Appreciate the fact that she shared some of his same interests like watching sports and even playing them. Snicker with pride over the way one tiny girl used her tongue and rapier wit to defend herself. And most of all, he finally saw her as more than the pig-tailed torment who'd tackled him so many times he'd vowed never to play football again. He looked at her and saw...perfection. *My mate.* And his wolf sighed in canine relief that the idiot human it was stuck with finally stopped being a dumbass.

Startled from his musings, he heard her reply. "I gave up on you as a mate. Too much work. And besides, you're grumpy. I don't need to wake up to that every day."

He frowned. "I am not grumpy."

"Are too."

"Am not."

"Are too."

"Children, behave!" shouted Naomi from the hall.

"Am not," he whispered.

She elbowed his injured side, and he sucked in a breath. "Ow! That wasn't nice."

"Pussy."

"Shrew."

She snickered. "Shrew? Really? That's the best you could come up with."

"You're really annoying sometimes, you know?"

"Only sometimes? I'll have to try harder then."

"Or you could shut up. You know, enjoy the sound of silence and rest your gums."

"Make me."

What possessed him, he didn't know. The scent of the cat still lingered on her. He'd not yet resolved what he wanted to do about her. Actually, he had, he wanted her, but he wanted to go about it slowly, cautiously. But still despite all that, he kissed her, a brief touch at first, which sent a jolt of awareness through him and made her gasp. He liked it, liked it a lot actually, and even better, she seemed to as well. So he kissed her again, slanting his mouth over hers, testing its fullness before tugging her lower lip between his for a suck. She parted her mouth, a small moan of need rolling into his. He thrust his tongue into the opening, ran it along the length of hers, tasted her, and wanted more.

Her hand crept up to touch his face, and he didn't miss her wince. It brought him back to sanity, but did nothing to curb his arousal. He pulled back. "Sorry. I shouldn't have done that."

"Why did I know you were going to say that?" she replied on a sigh.

"I didn't mean I regretted kissing you. That we're definitely going to have to do again, but first you need to heal. I don't want to be the jerk who takes advantage of you while you are lying injured in bed."

"Could have fooled me," Naomi said from the doorway. "Men. Always thinking with their little heads instead of their big ones. Now get out so she can sleep."

A mulish expression dropped over Francine's face and he could smell the coming fight. He verbally stepped in before it could erupt. "I'm staying. Besides, won't it make it easier if we're both in the same room to take care of?"

"I thought you weren't that injured," his sister said, narrowing her eyes in challenge.

Adopting a puppy dog face, he tried to look as pitiful as possible while beside him, Francine snickered. "I'm feeling kind of weak, actually. I think all that exertion has caught up. Francine won't mind if I nap beside her. Will you, Red?"

She let out a long-suffering sigh. "Fine. But I warn you right now, I've been told I'm a bed hog."

And boy, did that turn out to be the understatement of the century, Mitchell thought as she sprawled on her stomach across the mattress, the comforter tucked under her cheek while he held on by the tiniest sliver of mattress. However, despite the discomfort, he couldn't really say there was another place he'd rather be. The thought didn't frighten him as much as he expected.

Chapter Nine

Playing the card game, Asshole—which still made them giggle just as energetically as it did when they were kids—with Mitchell, Naomi along with whomever wasn't out searching for the hunter got tedious after a while. But, Francine couldn't deny that even as she missed Alejandro, she enjoyed spending time with Mitchell, the boy she remembered now a man with the same temper and twisted set of morals that let him cheat at cards, but think that his sister's BFF was off limits.

Or used to be off limits. True to his word, he'd not left her presence since her injury the previous morning, sleeping by her side, grumbling that she kicked in her sleep. His family took his presence as a given, not saying a word, which surprised Francine given his family weren't the types to curb their tongues. It seemed everyone assumed he'd taken his rightful spot. Francine might have thought it too except for one thing; he didn't say or do anything to make her think his newfound glued to her side status was permanent. Which really sucked.

She wanted to think he'd turned the corner when it came to his thinking of her, that he'd forgotten his idiotic obsession with treating her as his sister. Hard to pretend, though, when he did nothing to convince her that he saw her in a romantic light. He'd not tried a repeat of his kiss—not once—even though she'd woken a few times with his face mere inches from her, his eyes studying her intently as if she puzzled him. Yet, despite his lack of action, she could see the hunger in his gaze, and she caught him adjusting himself when he thought she wasn't looking, obviously aroused. She loved that she could cause such a reaction, hope blossoming that she'd finally get what her heart had forever desired.

However…even as she exulted over their burgeoning closeness, she worried about Alejandro and missed him. Funny how in his short time, he'd managed to snag a portion of her heart. Odder still how she saw nothing wrong with caring so strongly for another man while in bed with the one she'd always loved. *Naomi's right, I am a skank.* One who wasn't getting laid, unfortunately.

"What's got you looking so down, Red?" Mitchell asked, tweaking a curl, employing his new nickname for her.

What would he say if she said she needed some naked loving? Probably dive out of the window if past incidences were any indication. Maybe she should keep her lusty needs to herself. "Has anyone heard from Jag?" she asked.

"Nope, and I say good riddance to that. Maybe the alley cat's slunk back home."

Mitchell just couldn't resist the barbs about Alejandro. She elbowed him and he grunted. "Alejandro wouldn't do that. He said he'd come back." And despite her own trepidation that he'd gotten a taste and lost interest, a part of her believed him when he said he'd return.

"Like a cold sore."

"Don't be an ass, Mitchell. Despite what you think of him, he's been nothing but nice to me. Nicer than you've been I might add."

"What are you talking about? I'm here, aren't I, keeping you company and saving you from boredom?"

"And what about the five years previous to that?" she remarked dryly.

"I was busy?" he said with a hopeful lilt.

"Busy shagging skanks. And the only reason you're even talking to me again is because of Jag. At least he's never bowled people over to escape me." Although, Mitchell was doing better. He'd gone from one extreme to another, glued to her side if for reasons still vague to her.

"Can we stop talking about him?" Mitchell grumbled.

Oh ho, did she hear a hint of jealousy? What fun. "Why? I like talking about him, like how big and strong he is. What amazing eyes he has. Oh, and he does this wicked thing—"

A pillow slapped her on the head along with Mitchell's growled, "Enough. You like the cat. I get it. Now, change the subject."

"Are you jealous, Mitchy?" she bugged as she yanked the pillow off her head.

"Of course not."

Even she could hear the lie. She smiled to herself. "Fine. No more discussing Jag and how awesome he is. What do you want to do instead?" she asked as she gingerly rolled onto her back. The gunshot wound had closed, the skin knitting itself together, but still felt very tender. One of Mitchell's hands helped prop her as the other stuffed pillows behind her back.

"Wanna play cards again?" he asked. Done playing nursemaid, he leaned back.

"No. And I swear, if you try and make me, I'm going to hide the ace in a hole that you're not going to like."

"Testy, testy. Wanna watch some television?"

"It's eleven a.m., which means talk shows or reruns. No thanks." She didn't need to know who the father of the teenage girl's baby was. Seriously, how did people stomach those shows? And the Price Is Right just wasn't the same without Bob Barker.

"Okay, grouchy one, what do you want to do then?"

"Truth or dare." She blurted it out without even thinking. She immediately expected him to shoot the idea down. Once again, he surprised her.

"Okay, Red. You're on. Me first."

She frowned at him. "Why do you go first? I came up with the idea."

A smirk twisted his lips. "Which means I go first. Or do you want to arm wrestle for the privilege?"

He'd like that, wouldn't he? "Jerk. Go ahead, ask away. I've got nothing to hide."

He grinned. "Excellent. So what's it going to be, truth or dare, Red?"

"Truth." Her eyes dared him to do his worst.

"Are you really going to let the cat move in and share your bed?"

"Yes. He's a great cook and I liked sleeping with him. All night long. He's the one who complained I didn't share the bed well and that I stole all the covers." She presented him with an innocent smile that completely ignored his glower.

Mitchell growled. "You didn't answer the question. You know that's not what I meant."

"Then next time ask me properly because I answered the question. My turn. Truth or dare?"

"Truth."

She cackled. "Ooh, you're feeling brave, are you? Okay so answer this then, do you still see me as a sister?" Going after him with a big blazing truth gun, she almost held her breath waiting for the answer.

His eyes scrutinized her, and his answer, when it came, emerged slowly. "No. I most definitely don't think of you as a sister anymore." Her heart raced as she waited for him to say something more on the subject, but instead, he said, "Truth or dare?"

"Truth."

"Do you love the cat?"

Blinking at the blunt question, she didn't immediately reply. Honesty meant she couldn't avoid it, even if she knew he wouldn't like the answer. "I'm pretty sure I do." A blank mask dropped over his face, but she could see the tension in his body.

"Are you going to let him claim you?"

"My turn to ask a question," she said, stalling him. "Truth or dare?"

"Truth."

"Are you here just to protect me?"

"No."

He didn't elaborate and she glared at him. The jerk just grinned. "I love payback. My turn. Truth or dare?"

Having heard the question already, she avoided it. "Dare."

His brows shot up. "Aw, so that's how you're going to play, hmmm? Chicken. Okay then, I dare you to tell Naomi she's fat."

Francine snorted. "I already did that this morning when you were in the bathroom. She then told me I looked like a scraggly refugee. Come on, you can do better than that."

"Such a smart ass. You want something harder then? Fine, I dare you to kiss me."

"Seriously? Piece of cake, although, to spare my back, do you mind bending over so I can reach you?"

Chagrin flashed on his face and she almost laughed as he leaned over, his face hovering in front of hers. "If you want to change your mind it's—"

Plastering her mouth against his shut him up, and this time, her mind clear, her body rested, she could say without a shadow of a doubt he felt just as good as she recalled. Slanting her mouth over his, she nibbled the flesh, enjoying how his heart sped up and his breathing got more and more ragged. He pulled away first, swallowing hard, his eyes alight with passion, but he controlled himself, if with difficulty, the cords in his neck standing out. A quick glimpse down showed his hands clenched into fists. He still insisted on staying in control, it seemed. What a shame. She wondered how far she'd have to push him before he finally caved.

Her voice husky, she said, "My turn, truth or dare?"

He licked his lips, and a surge of lust roared through her as she realized how much she wanted that tongue—in her mouth, on her body, in her pussy. But Mitchell wasn't Alejandro. He required more coaxing.

"Dare?" He spoke the word it as if worried, and with good reason.

Tossing him a wicked grin, she pointed to her groin clad in track pants. His forehead wrinkled with incomprehension and she smiled wider.

"I want you to put your mouth on my crotch and blow."

"Are you out of your mind?"

"So I've been told. What's wrong? Are you turning down a dare? Pussy. Jag would do it in a heartbeat."

"But someone could come in. And you're hurt. And…"

She rolled her eyes. "I am really starting to think the rumors of you in the sack were false. I mean—Oh!"

The startled sigh escaped her as Mitchell placed his face between her thighs, his mouth against her sex. He blew and even filtered through her track pants, she felt the heat. And he didn't do it just once. No, he kept his mouth pressed on her, breathing at her, and even through the fabric, it aroused her. Melted her into a puddle of aching desire. And she craved more.

Shudders wracked her and a low moan vibrated through her, followed by another when he worked his lips against the fabric, tugging at her. Her fingers gripped his hair, and she ignored the twinge of discomfort in her wound as she rocked her hips against his face.

"Phone for you… Hey, pervert, that's my bed you're misbehaving in," Naomi screeched at her brother.

As if scalded, he rolled off the bed, the passion on his face warring with his red-cheeked embarrassment. As usual, he got mad and blamed someone else.

Pointing a finger at Francine, he stammered, "She made me do it. She dared me. Yell at her."

Naomi grinned at her. "Truth or dare?"

"Of course. Idiot thought he could beat me at it."

They both snickered while Mitchell scowled at them. "Did you want us for something other than causing trouble?" he growled.

"Oh yeah, phone call for Francine." Naomi waddled to the bed and handed over the cell phone. "It's Alejandro. Or should I say Jag, which I must say, is the coolest nickname ever. Javier won't admit it, but he's soooo jealous."

"Am not," Javier hollered from the hall.

"Don't worry, I'm sure we can come up with another kitty name for you, like Sylvester or Tom," she yelled back, grinning.

"Apparently, I'm not allowed to call him God in public, although he has no problem with it when we're alone."

Ethan lumbered in shaking his head, and swept his mate into his arms. "I apologize for her wayward tongue. The pregnancy hormones have made her crazier than she already was."

"Oh, teddy bear!" she snarled.

"Yes my delicate flower?" he said, placidly carrying her out.

"Don't you flower me. I resent being called crazy. I prefer straightforward."

Francine giggled. She loved seeing Naomi so relaxed with her men. *I'd love to have the same type of relationship with mine.* She'd almost forgotten the phone in her hand, but a tinny "Hello?" made her bring it to her ear.

"Alejandro! Are you okay?"

"Hey, baby. Miss me?"

"More than you deserve." She smiled as she said it, glad he'd called.

Mitchell crawled back on the bed. "Is that the cat? Ask him if he caught the hunter."

"Tell the dog, not yet."

"He heard you. Now, you didn't answer me, are you okay? When are you coming back?" It eased something in her to hear his voice, to know he'd not forgotten her.

"I'm fine if lonely and horny. The hunter seems headed back to my hometown so I've been following him. I'm hoping to corner him tonight, which means I should be back tomorrow sometime, the day after at the latest. What about you, though? How's your back?"

"Healing. They won't let me do anything," she grumbled.

"Ahh, poor baby. I'll try and get back soon so I can find ways to keep you *entertained*." His soft chuckle made her smile because she could so easily imagine what he meant.

"Pig," she said softly.

He laughed. "I miss you too. How are things with the dog?"

"They're going."

"I've got to say I'm surprised Mitchell hasn't used my absence to make his big move."

Peering over at Mitchell, who pretended not listen, she said, "We're making progress."

"In other words, he's dragging his heels instead of seducing you. Idiot. Better get him to hurry up because once I get back, you probably won't be allowed up for air for at least a day or so." That made Mitchell growl and leave the bed. Actually, he left the room entirely, his back a rigid board.

She sighed.

"I take it he left?"

"Of course he did. Progress doesn't mean he's ready to admit he has feelings for me even if every time you're mentioned he turns absolutely green."

"Has he at least kissed you yet?"

Francine blushed, tongue tied at the question. *Exactly what is the protocol to admitting to your lover that you've let another man kiss you?*

"I'll take your silence as a yes. I'll be damned. Looks like you might get what you've wanted, baby."

The surreal tenor of the conversation threw her for a loop. "How come you're so casual about this? Hell, even so encouraging? Most guys would be… Jealous and freakn'."

"And chance losing you? No thanks. I'm not blind or stupid. You've wanted Mitchell pretty much all your life. If I forced you to choose between us, there's a possibility I wouldn't win. Seems pretty dumb to act the part of jealous idiot, like a certain dog I know, given I know a three-way relationship can work. Just look at Naomi and her men. I don't see why we can't enjoy the same thing. Don't get me wrong, a part of me would love to strangle the dog and throw him off a cliff, but ultimately, it's what you need that counts. I'm not saying we won't have to make adjustments. But I'm willing. The bigger question is, can Mitchell cope?"

Remembering Mitchell's rigid countenance, she sighed. "Not likely."

"Don't sound so negative, baby. Fate wouldn't have picked us both if it didn't think it would work. But I do think it will be easier if he's already claimed you before I come back. Because no matter what he thinks or wants, I won't go another day without making you mine."

"You seem too sure I'm going to let you," she teased even as she knew she would, probably the moment they tumbled naked into bed.

"You forget, I know your sweet spots."

"I miss you," she whispered, just as Mitchell came back in the room holding two cans of pop.

"Me too, baby. Tell Mitchell to kiss you for me, and be prepared for the real thing sometime tomorrow. Dream of me."

"Bye." She hung up, sad and missing Alejandro, who, despite his short tenure in her life, left his mark.

Crouching at the side of the bed, Mitchell deposited the cans on the nightstand and peered at her. "Are you okay?"

"Yeah. He's almost caught the guy and should be back tomorrow."

"That's it?"

"Well, other than he misses me and wants to mark me, pretty much. Oh, he did also say to kiss me for him," she said saucily.

"Usually, I'd tell the cat where he can shove his orders, but this is one time I think I should do as he says," Mitchell murmured. He tilted her face for a kiss, but she put a hand up and held him off.

"Are you sure you want to do this? He's going to mark me when he gets back."

"And?"

She growled. "Fine. Make me say it. What are your intentions toward me, Mitchell?"

"Can't we just kiss?"

"And you talk about Jag being the seducer. At least he's offering me a future."

Clambering onto the bed first, nudging her in the process, Mitchell rolled onto his back and laced his hand behind his head. Then he let out a big sigh. "My intentions? Honestly? I don't know, Red. A part of me wants you so fucking bad, it hurts."

"So jerk one off in the shower."

He tossed a glare her way. She grinned. "Not just that kind of pain, smart ass," he grumbled. "And for your information I have, numerous times and it's not working."

"Oh." She almost gulped at his roundabout admission that he cared. "So what's the problem then?"

"You're planning to let that cat mark you and become your mate."

She wouldn't lie, not for something this important. "Yes, I am. It doesn't mean I don't want you too. I still want you as much as I ever did, Mitchell."

Another loud sigh emerged from him, deflating him so that he slumped. "And I'm realizing more and more that I want you as well, even if parts of me are still reconciling the new sexy you with the little girl I used to know. But, that part is getting easier and easier. What I don't know is if I can share. The idea of a threesome… If we're being honest, then I have to admit, it kind of wigs me out."

Great, Mitchell finally admitted to caring for her—and that he found her hot, which totally rocked—and she was chasing him away because she'd fallen in love with a second man. Why couldn't her love life have stayed simple?

She placed her hand on his thigh. "Nobody's saying if you both claim me that we need to have three-way sex. Some ménages do, others don't."

"How the hell would you know about threesomes?"

A smile crossed her lips. "Naomi's situation is not the first I've encountered. My aunt Belinda actually had three mates. My great grandma Josephine had a pair. You could say it kind of runs in the family. And while my mom used to cover my ears whenever my aunt decided to relate some particularly racy exploit, great grandma was very prim and proper despite her ménage marriage. My great grandpas each had their own rooms and from what I understood, took turns. Heck, they even had a calendar with a schedule, which I'll admit I didn't clue in to for years."

"That's fucked up."

"Maybe to some people, but it worked for them. And it could work for us. I would never make you do something you're not comfortable with. If having you means only enjoying hot one-on-one sex with screaming orgasms, then I think I can manage." She grinned at him. "Don't you know? I'd do just about anything to have you as my mate?"

"Don't remind me. I still shudder at the smell of watermelon bubblegum."

She thumped a fist on thigh. "Jerk. Now is not the time to discuss how you crushed my childhood dreams."

"And what are your adult ones?" he asked, grabbing her pummeling fist and enveloping it in his hand.

She stilled. "My fantasy, which I'll admit has recently been upgraded, involves being mated to two wonderful, yet different men, who worship the ground I walk on, and do totally wicked things to my body."

"What if I wanted to do nice things?"

"As long as you use your tongue and cock, I think I can manage."

"Francine, that is vulgar."

"Oh don't be such a prude. Don't forget, I used to spy on you when you were younger and you've said way worse than that."

"You are so asking for a spanking," he growled.

"Why Mitchell, I never knew you were into kink," she replied, batting her eyes lashes.

He groaned and covered his face with his hands, muttering, "Why me?"

She giggled. "Oh admit it. Life with me would definitely never bore you."

"No, but I can see sore knuckles and broken noses in my future if you insist on claiming that cat."

"You'll heal. Besides, think of the fun you'll have when I kiss your booboo's better."

"You have an answer for everything, don't you?"

Tapping her chin, she pretended to think. "Yes, yes I do. But you," she said, fixing him with a stare, "have every excuse not to."

"Fine. Let's say I, um, did claim you. And the seducer did too. You really think we could make it work?" he asked, skepticism in his tone. "I don't know if I could keep myself from killing the cat if I saw him touching you."

"Which is why we could do it just like my great grandma did. Okay, that sounds so wrong and is not the mental image I want right now."

Mitchell chuckled. "What, you don't like thinking of your great grandpa chasing your squealing great grandma around the kitchen while your other grandpa watches, waiting his turn?"

A moue of distaste crossed her face. "It excites me as much as I'm sure the thought of your father doing your mother on the dining room table does."

"They've never done that," he adamantly replied.

She arched a brow. "Oh really? Tell that to the ass marks Naomi had to polish off the surface wearing rubber gloves."

He blanched and she grinned triumphantly.

"Can we change the subject?"

"Sure. I believe we were talking about coming up with a schedule so that I could have both you and Alejandro in my life."

"If I choose to mark you. I'm still on the fence."

She jabbed her elbow in his gut and he grunted. "Stop lying or I'll tell your mama and she'll get the soap."

"You really are annoying sometimes," he grumbled.

"It's part of my charm. Admit it. You enjoy it."

"Will not."

"Liar. Do you prefer Ivory or Irish Spring?"

"Fine. Fine. It's kind of enjoyable. Happy now?"

"Yes, I am," she said, beaming at him. "So, what do you think of my idea?"

"This is the most fucked up conversation ever. I assume you mean your suggestion of taking turns being with you? You'd go for that?"

"If it meant having you as well as Alejandro, then yes. I can compromise. I want you, Mitchell. I've wanted you for a long time. I never imagined, though, I'd have to share you, especially with another man."

"Okay that sounds gross when you put it that way."

She laughed. "You know what I mean. But it does depend on you. Alejandro will claim me when he returns."

"If he returns."

"When he returns," she restated. "I guess the only question left is, will you claim me too?"

"I—" He paused. His brow knitted in confusion while his eyes spoke of longing. As for his cock. Oh yes, definite tenting action.

"You can say it," she coaxed. "I won't bite—hard—until you do."

"I—"

A shriek sounded. "Naomi!" they both exclaimed, him with a note of relief. Mitchell helped her up and supported her as they made their way out of the bedroom to the living room where Naomi paced, ranting at the top of her lungs.

"Unfucking believable. How fucking dare she? That ho! That bloody, dirty skank. I'm going to rip—Oh, hey there, Francine. What are you doing up? You're supposed to be in bed."

Her possessed friend pasted a fake smile meant to look reassuring on her face, but rage glistened in her eyes. Francine, plopping onto the couch, careful not to lean back, would have none of it. "What's got your panties in a twist?"

"I'm not wearing any. So nothing."

"Eeew!" Mitchell exclaimed.

"Oh shut it, crotch sniffer," his sister snarled. "No one's talking to you."

"Naomi, be nice!" Javier said in a firm tone. "It's not his fault you're upset. And besides, you know he's going to go ballistic when he finds out. Won't that be fun?"

"Find out what?" Mitchell asked, sitting on the arm of the couch beside Francine.

"That fucking skanky ho with the slutty—" Javier put his hand over Naomi's mouth, silencing her, not quite managing to hide the wince when she bit him.

Ethan shook his head. "She's a little upset."

"Do you think?" Francine drawled, wondering what had Naomi in such a tizzy. Probably some groupie hitting on one of her mates again. This far in her pregnancy, with her hormones running wild, it didn't take much for Naomi's jealous green monster to come out swinging.

Javier, though, shot her theory to hell with his next words. "The hunter who shot Mitchell wasn't the person who shot Francine."

Ballistic didn't even come close to describing Mitchell when he found out who had. Francine quite enjoyed seeing him all riled up. It pleased her inner bitch even more. However, the method of discovery, AKA her trashed apartment, pissed her right off. *Someone's head is going to roll.*

Chapter Ten

Irritated and longing to go home, the new home he'd discovered in Francine's arms, made Alejandro impatient. For the last two days, he'd followed the hunter's sloppy trail. First missing him by minutes at the scuzzy motel he'd checked out of, the location courtesy of a receipt he'd found snagged on a branch in the tree the bastard perched in. The female clerk at least—after a little persuasion, AKA a smile from him—divulged not only the truck's plate number for his prey but also the make and color of it, which as it turned out, Javier had if he'd bothered asking before running off . What a surprise, the hunter drove a big ass, red pickup truck. *Stupid redneck.* Most people thought hillbillies and rednecks were an American phenomena. He had news for them, Canada had its fair share of crass, belligerent types who shot anything that moved. But, even he had to admit, their daughters were raunchy in bed.

Stereotypes aside, he jumped on the highway, the clerk having mentioned the man said he was heading home to deal with his daughter. On his bike, it was a simple matter to weave in and out of traffic, slowing down before overpasses to avoid the inevitable radar traps. Late afternoon, he caught up to his prey on the highway. He felt like thanking the bastard for owning such a distinctive red pickup truck with the redneck sticker that read "Keep Honking Asshole, I'm Loading My Gun." He meant to follow the vehicle until it stopped for either fuel, food, or sleep, but his fucking bike began to wobble, forcing him to pull off and deal with a flat fucking tire. Lucky for him, the tow truck driver knew a place to fix him up and get back on the road, but he lost two precious hours. Even worse, he'd lost the redneck he chased. Thus far, the stupid human had traveled in a straight line, keeping his trek to the highway that led back to his home town. Alejandro decided he'd have to trust the idiot would keep on his path, meaning he'd rendezvous with him in the morning on his home turf.

Tired, wind beaten, and with a cold rain starting to fall, he decided rather than risk road rash, he would pull into a motel off the highway. And then he finally got a stroke of luck, seeing a big, honking red truck in the parking lot.

Thank you, Lady Luck, for that one.

Sniffing around the vehicle, he made sure of his quarry first, scenting the lingering traces of bear, a hunter's perfume, and the familiar tang of the daughter, whose feminine scent was the last he'd inhaled before meeting his Francine.

Kicking in the motel room door, he startled the balding fellow lounging on the bed watching television. With a curse, the tubby hunter rolled off the bed, scrambling for his jacket and withdrawing a gun. Like that would stop him.

Enraged, not at the temerity of the human, but what he'd done to his precious mate, Alejandro leapt across the room and knocked it from his grasp. Ramming his forearm against the human's throat, he used this as leverage and shoved him into the wall. But that wasn't

155

enough. He lifted him until the hunter gurgled, his fingers clawing desperately at his arm.

Alejandro's lips curled back over his teeth in a vicious snarl. "Fucking prick. Not so brave without your gun, are you? I can forgive you for shooting the wolf. I've had the urge myself. But shooting at a woman through her window in the back? For that, you die."

The hunter's head tried to shake in a puny attempt at denial. Curious as to what lame excuse the bastard thought to spout, Alejandro eased the pressure to let him speak his final words before he killed him.

"Not me," croaked the sweating human.

A cold smile danced over his lips at the poor attempt at rebuttal. "Are you denying you shot the wolf and the redhead?"

"Shot the wolf, but I left right after. I didn't shoot any redhead."

Truth rang in the human's words, and Alejandro frowned. Removing his arm, Alejandro let his prey drop. The man slumped to the floor, gasping and clutching his throat.

"Start from the beginning and tell me what you've done, starting with following me. You know what I am."

He nodded his head. "I saw you in the woods behind my place. You're not human."

"No shit. So that gives you the right to follow me and threaten the lives of people I know and love?"

"You seduced my daughter," the redneck replied in a blustery tone as he sat up.

156

"She's twenty freakn' five. She bloody well seduced me."

The hunter turned beet red. "She's still my little girl and it fucking burned me to know she'd slept with some animal."

"So you tried to track me down."

"I didn't try, I did. I found out where you lived and I saw you leaving. I followed."

"Pretty long fucking trip."

"Yeah, well, I was kind of pissed."

"And then?"

The human shrugged. "I saw you visiting that house with the pregnant gal. I watched for a few hours, but I needed some supplies and left for just a little bit. When I came back, you were gone. I almost went home that night, but I called my daughter and she was so pissed at me."

"So you came back the next day?"

"Not right away. I almost went home. I drove around for a bit, but then my damned daughter called again PMSing so off I went back to watch for you. But you didn't show up. I came better prepared that time, though, and found myself a spot in a tree, and then that fucking wolf showed up."

"Okay, this story is getting long and tedious. You shot the wolf, ran away, and then found me the next morning, right?"

"No. When I was running away, I heard all the fucking animals coming, and I got in my fucking truck and left."

"Not too far you didn't because lo and behold, I caught up to you. Made a pit stop perhaps on your way home, maybe to shoot someone."

"No. I went and got royally fucking drunk. After I slept it off, I called my daughter cell's phone only to find out she'd gone to your fucking ranch to warn them I was hunting you and then couldn't leave."

"My family kept her prisoner?" The news surprised him.

The human crossed his arms and scowled. "Not according to her. Apparently, she didn't want go. So I demanded to speak to someone there and your brother Ignacio came on the line and said they'd mated and that I'd better get my ass home if I wanted to see her again."

"I see." Alejandro mentally winced, wondering how Ignacio felt about Alejandro dipping his wick into his mate's honey pot. Probably not too happy. It would make Christmas interesting for sure.

"After I hung up, I left for home. How could I not? Felicia means everything to me. And I can't go around killing you and your buddies if she's being held hostage."

Alejandro dragged the man to his feet and hugged him.

"What the fuck are you doing?" Panic threaded his tone.

"Welcoming you to the family, of course," Alejandro said, releasing him with a chuckle.

"What are you talking about?"

"Congratulations, your daughter is now married to an animal. My brother. And trust me, I'm a pussycat compared to him."

"So you're not going to kill me?"

"And have my brother hunt me down to please his mate? No. Besides, all you did was shoot a mangy dog. Can't fault a man for that." On the heels of his words, though, realization dawned just as his phone rang.

Answering Javier's call, he blurted, "It wasn't the hunter that shot Francine." And he needed to get back ASAP to protect her from whoever still roamed at large.

"We know."

"You do. Who is it? I'm going to kill the bastard."

"It's a she."

"What?" Alejandro sat down hard as the hunter, and newest honorary family member, dashed to the bathroom and locked himself in.

"Chris went over to her place before lunch— "

"And you're just calling me now?" he yelled.

"We were busy. Now do you want to hear what happened or not?"

"Fine. But you have got to do something about your communication skills, brother, because this is twice now you've screwed me."

"Yeah, I know. Trust me. I had to listen to an earful from my wife. Anyway, as I was saying, Chris went to get some stuff for her to wear and found Francine's place trashed with the word 'whore' plastered all over the place."

"Oh fuck. Which of my psycho ex-girlfriends did it?" he moaned, cradling his head in his hands.

"Not yours, Mitchell's. Seems his ex, Jenny, wasn't too happy he ditched her for Francine. She's the one who shot her and trashed her apartment."

Unfreakn' believable. "And where is the crazy bitch now?"

"No one seems to know, but we've got the shifter authorities looking for her along with Naomi's brothers."

"What happens when we find her?"

A loud sigh was Javier's answer.

"We can't let her go free for this," Alejandro growled. "She needs to be punished. She shot Francine. My mate."

"Almost mate."

"Don't argue semantics with me. I want justice."

"Something will be done, but you know they won't put her to death. Especially with Francine recovered."

"I've got an idea, why don't we shoot her in the back, too? See how she likes it." His sarcastic reply pleased his feral side, which demanded vengeance still for the wrong done to his woman.

"Now you sound like Naomi."

"I knew I liked your wife. How's Francine taking it?" Was she crying, terrified, angry…

"She's still laughing her ass off."

"What?"

"You have to see it to believe it. She's pissed, don't get me wrong, but she's cracking jokes about it and giggling like she's on drugs."

He frowned. "What kind of jokes?"

Javier lowered his tone. "Um, well, the first thing she said when she heard who'd trashed her place was, 'Anorexic slut was probably looking for cookies.' So then Mitchell says, 'Red, you do realize she's the one who shot you?' and do you know what your mentally unbalance woman said?"

"I'm afraid to ask," Alejandro replied as he rubbed the bridge of his nose.

"She said, get this, 'Hey, Naomi, you might have gotten shot at because someone wanted your men, but I got shot because I stole someone's man. In your face!' I think she's still in shock."

A chuckle, more of relief than humor, escaped him. "No, that sounds about right. Keep her out of trouble, would you? I'm on my way back. Oh, and that hunter I was chasing..."

"Yeah? Did you find him and take care of him?"

"Not exactly. He's now family. His daughter is mated to Ignacio."

"No fucking way! Damn. I'll bet Mama's pissed."

Alejandro winced. Knowing how his Spanish mother felt about hunters, pissed probably didn't even come close to describing her reaction.

They said good-bye and hung up. Pocketing his phone, Alejandro glanced around and noted the human still hid in the bathroom.

"I'm off now. Say hi to the family for me, would you?" he said loudly before exiting the motel. What a surprise, the hunter didn't reply. Christmas would definitely be interesting. But he had other things on his mind.

Time to go home, to Francine.

* * * *

Despite her friend's protestations, Francine insisted on seeing the damage at her place. Somehow, though, hearing it secondhand just didn't compare to seeing it in person. The moment she walked in her door and saw the devastation, the jokes she'd cracked the whole way over—such as, "I hope she didn't mess with my dildo collection"—dwindled as disbelief took over.

Jenny hadn't just tossed the place, she'd ruined it. From the slashed cushions on her couch to the smashed china and lamps, the crazy bitch had left nothing intact. She'd dumped all her clothes on her mattress and poured bleach on them, shredded her pictures, written on the walls… Everywhere she looked, Francine saw devastation and meaningless violence. Against her. And her only mistake? Wanting the man she knew belonged to her.

While Naomi ranted and raved about how she'd tear the bitch's claws out one by one, Mitchell following suit, Francine exited via the back door of her townhouse and sank onto her tiny concrete patio, chest heaving and her eyes brimming with tears. A body settled beside her, and she turned to see Javier, his dark gaze so reminiscent of Alejandro, she almost started crying. She missed him so much.

"It's only stuff, Francine," he said softly.

"I know," she sniffed. "It's not that, well it is, but it's—" How to explain the violation? The unfairness? "How could she?"

"Jealousy will do strange things to people," he replied.

She chuckled wetly. "I'll say. You know what really sucks, though? Is she punished me, and yet, I don't even have Mitchell."

"Like fuck you don't," was the growl from behind her. "Can you give us a minute?" Mitchell asked.

Giving her a quick one-armed hug first, Javier then stood and said to Mitchell in a menacing tone, "Don't fuck up."

"Why does everyone keep saying that?" Mitchell grumbled, taking Javier's place beside her. Then he went one step further and dragged her onto his lap. She stiffened at first, but then relaxed as he wrapped his arms around her, cuddling her into him. She sighed, a sound repeated by her wolf, and relaxed in his embrace.

"I. Am. So. Sorry." Each word came out alone and so coated in chagrin she couldn't help a weak laugh.

163

"It's not your fault. I guess maybe you are as good as they say in the sack if Jenny's willing to murder me just to get back together with you."

"This isn't funny, Red. She could have killed you and all because I'm a fucking idiot who refused to see what was in front of me."

"And what did you not see?" she asked softly.

"I want you. Hell, I think I need you."

"You're just saying that because you feel sorry for me and guilty about what happened."

He sighed. "No, I'm saying it because it's true. For years I let you scare me into staying away. Avoiding you became second nature."

"Great. That makes me feel soooo much better," she drawled sarcastically.

"Smart ass. Do you know why I did it?"

"Because I had cooties?"

"No."

"Because of my freckles."

"No, I actually really like those."

"It's because my ass is too wide."

"No, you idiot. Your ass is freakn' amazing. No, the reason why I avoided you was because deep down inside, when you told me we belonged together, a part of me knew it was true. And it scared the fuck out of me. I honestly saw you as a little sister, so when I started feeling things for you, things you expected and accepted, I freaked and ran."

"Mitchell?"

"Yes."

"You are an idiot," she solemnly stated. Not an easy feat given her heart raced a mile a minute and her body tingled all over with anticipation. Her inner bitch had no such restraint and yipped at her, demanding she bite him before he changed his mind.

A rumble shook his chest. "I know I am, Red."

"So now that we've ascertained the fact that I am the smart one, what happens next?"

"I claim you, that is, if you'll still have me, dumb genes and all."

"And Alejandro?"

"Yeah, well, I won't say that I'm happy about sharing you with a feline, but so long as he keeps out of my face, I'll deal with it. For you."

Okay, so it wasn't as warm and fuzzy as she would have liked. It was still more than she could have ever expected. She'd finally gotten her man. "Kiss me," she demanded.

At her request, he immediately shifted her in his lap to face him, and she tilted her chin up, welcoming the soft touch of his lips, instant heat warming her. Then giddy joy—mixed with relief—flooded her. *Mitchell's going to claim me!* The dream of so long would happen.

Her arms crept up to lace around his neck, her fingers toying with the ends of his hair as she opened her mouth before the probing insistence of his tongue. Wet, wild, and filled with the promise of pleasure to come, it figured someone would interrupt it.

"You owe me twenty bucks," Naomi exclaimed from right behind them. "Told you he'd come to his senses before Alejandro came back."

"Ha. He hasn't marked her yet, so no money," retorted Ethan.

Mitchell and Francine broke apart and turned to peer at Naomi and her mates.

"What?" her best friend asked, trying to look innocent and failing.

"You wagered on me claiming Francine?" Mitchell asked.

"Well, yeah. If it makes you feel better, I knew you'd come to your senses. Javier here thought you'd hold out a while longer."

"Are you sure you want to belong to this family?" Mitchell whispered to her loudly.

"Yes." *More than anything.*

Intimate moment interrupted, Francine let Naomi take charge of getting her townhouse cleaned and her stuff replaced. Thankfully, her insurance, a small company also run by shifters, would cover most of the costs, with Mitchell insisting on covering the difference. Apparently, living at home, he'd managed to save up, which would come in handy, because as Francine peered about her small living space, it quickly became evident that living here with two larger than life males would have its challenges, especially with Mitchell only accepting Alejandro's role grudgingly.

166

But she'd deal with that hurdle when they came to it. First, she needed to get Mitchell alone so he could mark her before he got cold feet and changed his mind again. *Okay, that's a lie. I don't think he's going to be running again.* She, on the other hand, had a fire in her pussy that needed tending, and she knew just the man to put it out.

Chapter Eleven

The moon had just begun to peek over the tree tops when Francine finally convinced Mitchell go for a run in the woods. He'd tried to talk her out of it, arguing for the last two hours that he wanted her to go back to bed and rest. She ignored his order. Actually, she laughed at him, and in the face of her giggles, so much better than her moroseness of earlier at her town house, he couldn't say no. Nor could he throw her over his shoulder caveman style and drag her back to bed. Although, that idea did have merit, especially given the ropes they'd used to tie him down when trying to keep him abed still remained attached to his broken headboard and footboard. However, the walls in his house were thin, and he somehow doubted he'd be able to keep his hands off her if he had her trussed spread eagle on his bed. And while he didn't know if she was a screamer or not, Mitchell already knew he was noisy. Besides, knowing his mother, she'd be so happy he'd finally given in to fate, she'd probably stand outside his bedroom shouting pointers to make sure he didn't disappoint her new daughter-in-law.

So it was the woods, or…the woods. She'd left him no choice with her insistence that she needed to let her beast stretch.

"Are you sure you can do this?" Mitchell asked once again, unable to completely curtail his concern that Francine would over tax herself. Ever since he'd found out she'd gotten shot, he'd lived in a state of anxiety. Knowing how close he'd come to losing her made him realize so many things, like how he didn't want to go without seeing her anymore. Actually, in an abrupt one-eighty, he didn't know if he could go a single day without having her smiling or teasing him. And he knew his body would probably explode if he didn't get to sink into her soon.

Knowing she'd gotten shot because of him…God, the guilt. He understood Alejandro's need now to make things right. The same feeling made him want to hunt Jenny down and make her pay for her actions, girl or not. But at the same time, he couldn't leave Francine alone without protection. He'd have to bide his time until Alejandro returned. However, before the cat did, he needed to do something first. Something long overdue.

Their time together had made him realize so many things; first and foremost, he loved her. Loved the feisty girl he'd known as a child, and loved even more the fiery woman she'd become. No longer did thoughts of her as a sister plague him, because honestly, seeing Naomi alongside her as they organized the clean up just showcased the differences. Buried deep inside, he discovered the real reason he'd run all those years and it wasn't because he had brotherly thoughts. It was because he didn't and he feared what that meant.

Turns out I am a big, yellow-bellied coward. Because of his unwillingness to accept the truth, he'd forced her to turn to other men, men she'd slept with, who'd touched that curvy body, a body that could have belonged to him alone had he owned the courage to admit his feelings. Fuck, that pissed him off. And explained even more things like why he got so mad at her prom when he caught her and that kid in his car, the windows fogged up. He saw the flush in her cheeks, smelled the virgin blood, and he lost his mind. He almost killed her boyfriend that night, not truly understanding his rage, attributing it to the fact she was like family. Of course, he never hurt Naomi's first as bad. Nor had he gone after Naomi's other boyfriends like he had with Francine's when he came across them. Even then, despite not understanding why, he'd been jealous and freakn'.

The past couldn't rearrange itself, even with hindsight, but he could affect the future, claim it and her, forging new and beautiful memories. It just sucked that his refusal to see what he had under his nose now meant he had to share and with a cat of all things. It made him wonder if he'd accepted her years ago, whether Alejandro would have ever stood a chance. *Or was she always destined for two, the mating fever not truly affecting me until Alejandro came into her life.* It would certainly explain a lot, such as how he'd managed to fight claiming her for so long.

A fight that stopped tonight.

Staring down at her petite frame, the pair of them alone finally for the first time—except for the curious eyes he was sure spied from the house—anticipation made his mouth dry—and his cock hard. At Francine's behest, they were going to shift into their beasts and go for a run. What she didn't know, but probably suspected, was somewhere in those woods, probably in that sweet clearing with the soft grass, he would make love to her, and claim not just her body, but her heart and soul. Maybe if he made her come enough times, she'd start forgiving him for acting like such an ass all those years.

Despite his pleasurable plans, though, he worried that she'd not yet recovered enough. Hence his repeated statement of, "Maybe we should wait until you're stronger."

"Stop molly coddling me. I'm not some delicate freakn' flower, not like someone I know." She yelled the last bit, and Mitchell was sure he heard his sister, one of the hiding audience, snort. "For the last time, I'll be fine. Besides, the full moon is out and my wolf is demanding I let her out. It will help me regain the last of my strength."

Just over three days of rest and his wound just showed as a puckered scar, but Francine was a girl, and smaller to boot. The urge to coddle her remained. "I don't know if this is such a good idea."

With a snort of disgust, she yanked at the hem of her shirt, tugging it up past creamy white flesh. He averted his gaze out of habit and heard her laughter. "Too late for cold feet, Mitchell. Either you join me, or I take you right here and now. Think Naomi will give us pointers?"

"You're bossy."

"So I've been told. Just so you know, I like to tell you what to do in the bedroom too."

For some reason, the idea of his little Red giving him orders, like "Lick me," "Fuck me," or just plain, "Give me your cock to suck" excited him and made him rock freakn' hard. "You won't be able to say much if I've got my dick stuffed in your mouth," he retorted, the dirty words he'd thought slipping out by accident. Or not.

A delighted, husky chuckle erupted from her, and standing there in only a bra, her overly plump breasts spilling out of the cups, the rounded softness of her belly just peeking over her the waistband of her pants, he realized he'd never been so happy or aroused in his life.

Wait, when she pulled at the clasp of her bra, and let her glorious breasts jiggle free, her nipples hardening into points, okay, now he was the happiest and most aroused ever. He actually might have a drooled a bit. His tongue, he managed to keep in his mouth—for now—instead of panting. Another thing he found himself thankful for? She had her back to the house so Chris and his other brothers weren't seeing her glorious perfection. He'd hate to have to rip their eyes from their skulls. Mama would probably freak if he did.

"Are you going to just stand there and stare, because I'll have you know, I'm really looking forward to watching you strip. I want to see if you're as big as they say."

God but she goaded him at every turn. Teased him into wanting her even as he tried to take it slow and respect her. It seemed she didn't want that, though. And, truthfully, with his cock aching, her breasts teasing, and the wild scent of her arousal rising, he wondered if he could find the will to wait until they reached the clearing. Screw the eyes in the windows. He wanted her right here and now. *Remember the audience.*

"You know my family is watching."

"Oh please. Like they haven't seen you naked."

Naked, yes. Naked with a ten foot aching pole stretching from his groin, no. "Since you're so eager to get buff, then why don't you go first?" Too late, he realized the challenge he'd thrown her. She, of course, didn't even hesitate.

Showing no modesty whatsoever, her hands went right to the waistband of her pants and she shimmied them down over her rounded hips to display a skimpy pair of bikini panties that just covered her thatch. Moisture pooled in his mouth as he imagined burying his face in the fiery curls that surely matched the mop on her head.

"Wanna see the back? It's a thong," she taunted.

A thong? That meant… shit. Even with her back to the house, she was giving his brothers an eyeful. *Mine, ours,* his wolf agreed. Just as jealous as his beast, Mitchell swept her into his arms and carried her into the dark seclusion of the forest behind his parents' house.

"What are you doing?"

"My brothers don't need to see what's mine."

She laughed, a beautiful, carefree sound. "You do know your brothers have seen my bare ass before, right? Heck, just last summer, when I went cottaging with Naomi and Chris, we went skinny dipping in the lake."

Mental note to self: kill his little brother. Later. Right now, he needed to get some of his chafing clothes off.

Putting her down first, he stepped back and almost chuckled himself when her laughter abruptly cut off and all because he stripped his shirt off. She'd seen his chest before. Heck, they'd spent the last few days in bed together with him pretty much half naked. But now, with anticipation and arousal peppering the air, she regarded him with something akin to awe—and hunger. *Beautiful, arousing hunger, for me.*

Soft fingers stroked down his chest, circling around his pecs. "Nice," she murmured. Her digits kept moving until they hit his waistband, her deft fingers unsnapping his pants and pushing them down before he could form a coherent thought.

His erection tented his briefs, and she cupped him, squeezing his girth while he could only tremble, looking for a way to remain a little aloof. He struggled to find even an iota of his usual control, enough that he wouldn't throw her to the ground and ravish her.

"I thought you wanted to run," he gasped as she kneaded him through the stretched fabric.

"I do." She released him and stepped back, her head tilting back to give him a naughty smile. "I just wanted to make sure you had incentive to chase." With a flick of her hand and a wiggle of her hips, her panties slid down. Before he had time to fully admire the view, she let her animal take over, her body contorting and reshaping until a small wolf with a silky coat of russet stood in front of him. With a yip, she bounded off, and Mitchell quickly stripped and changed into his own shaggy beast before chasing.

Ghosting through the woods on sure paws, the anxiety of the last few days, the mind-boggling mess of his emotions, everything melted away—except for his desire. The more he chased the fleet-footed she-wolf, the more his blood heated and his excitement grew. When he caught her, there would be no hesitation or doubt. He'd claim her. Sink his cock into her while she stared into his eyes, and as she climaxed, he'd bite her, marking her in the old fashioned way, making her his.

The thought spurred him to move even faster, herding her flitting shape to the location he'd selected. When she finally dashed into the open clearing, he followed right on her heels, and then stumbled as he tried not to slam into her smaller frame. Yipping, his wolf chastised her only to shut up as his mind filtered the sounds they heard. It seemed his clearing of choice was already taken. And despite the fact they knew they must have an audience, the foursome on the grass didn't stop what they were doing.

Backing away, he and Francine moved back to the shelter of the woods, both of them riveted by the scene before them. For a man who'd never thought much of ménages before, he seemed to be running into them an awful lot lately. Worst, he recognized the woman in the clearing, a daughter to one of his mother's friends. One of her lovers, an old high school football team mate. Not that their identities made a difference. Anyone could have been a part of the fleshy tangle of limbs and he would have stared, mesmerized.

A head butted his side, and he peered down to see Francine's smaller beast leaning against him, her breathing rapid, the musk of her arousal perfuming the air around him. She felt the same fascination as he did with the undulating group. It made his hunger explode. He couldn't help shifting back into his human form. He ran his fingers through her silky fur, a fur that shivered then disappeared under his touch until he stroked smooth skin.

Standing, her head barely reaching his chin, she pressed her naked frame against him and whispered, "Is it wrong that I want to stare at them?"

Wrong? Never. He couldn't admit it aloud, but he'd always enjoyed watching people being intimate, a fetish he'd discovered in high school when he came across a girl giving a buddy of his a BJ under the bleachers during a school dance. He'd been unable to tear himself away, just like he'd stayed to watch Francine when Alejandro bounced her on his cock. Sometimes the role of audience could titillate almost as much as that of participant. Of course, only one thing could make it better. Sharing it with the woman he wanted, a naked, very horny one who pressed her buttocks up against his thighs, her head tilting back against his shoulder, a soft sigh trembling through her frame as she kept her eyes glued to the erotic scene before them.

Mitchell slipped an arm around her waist, her heated flesh so soft against him.

"Touch me," she whispered. "Cup my tits and play with them while I watch."

Heaven had found him. Obeying her orders made him almost explode, his prick nudging the crevice of her ass as his hands strayed up her rib cage to handle her plump breasts. He kneaded them, squeezing the heavy weights, something she seemed to enjoy because she rotated her buttocks against him, rubbing against his prick.

"Don't neglect my nipples."

As if. He stroked his thumbs over her already erect peaks, rubbing their pointed tips. She moaned, a low sound full of need.

In the clearing, as if their hidden watching spurred them on, the action got more frantic. They placed the woman on her hands and knees, and while she sucked on one cock, another plowed her pussy. The third stood off to the side, stroking his cock, waiting his turn.

"Oh God, that looks like so much fun," his naughty Red murmured.

He didn't disagree. The female sure seemed to enjoy herself and the males didn't seem to mind sharing in the least. Actually, they seemed quite aroused by the simple act of watching each other.

Slipping his hands from her breasts, he took the initiative instead of waiting for her command, eager to see if she felt as wet as he imagined. Sifting his fingers through her curls to her sex, he groaned at the evidence of her heated readiness. Moisture coated his fingers as he slid them over and around her lips, the slickness lubing his finger to rub over her clit.

She let out a sound between a groan and cry, and panted, "More."

He dipped a finger into her sex, the damp walls of her channel squeezing his penetrating digit. His breath caught at the tight heat he encountered. God, how good it would feel around his cock.

Apparently, the same idea occurred to her because her hand reached behind to stroke him. "Fuck me, Mitchell," she whispered. "I need to feel you inside me. Taking me."

"Shouldn't we go somewhere else?" He knew once he sank into her, he'd lose himself. Forget everything around him, even the foursome in the clearing. But then again, an audience to his claiming of her? Talk about the ultimate in taboo pleasure.

"I want them to hear us," Francine whispered as if reading his mind. "I want them to know they've turned us on. Let them see you fucking me." And with those titillating words, she bent over, exposing herself to him. Even in the darkness, with his enhanced eye sight, he could see the moisture glistening on her sex, the invitation to sink himself into her depths and find bliss.

Only an idiot would refuse.

He'd been stupid for long enough.

Grasping his cock, he rubbed it against her, wetting the head of his shaft before pushing the crown into her. Sweet freakn' heaven. Her channel clutched him tight, and he stopped a moment to enjoy the exquisite feel of her. Francine, though, apparently had reached the end of her patience.

"Stop making me wait, dammit. I've waited long enough." She rammed herself back against him, sheathing him quickly and fiercely. Mitchell couldn't prevent the yell that burst from him. Fuck, that felt good.

He dug his fingers into her ass cheeks, determined to control the pace lest he come too quick. But his feisty Red had other ideas as she rocked back and forth, sucking his length in and out of her pussy, her low moans constant as she set the pace, a rhythm that got faster and faster.

Mitchell just hung on for the ride, his body slapping into hers with a fleshy smack, over and over, the tight glove of her sex bringing him to the edge…

A ripple went through her channel, squeezing him in undulating waves, and a low scream vibrated from her as she came. Pulling her body up, their bodies intimately meshed, he bent until his face was buried against her upper shoulder. His hips held the pistoning rhythm as she came. His own climax hit and with a roar of "Mine!" he shot his seed into her as he sank his teeth into her shoulder, marking her as his.

* * * *

Was there such a thing as too much pleasure? If so, she'd found it as her vision saw stars, her heart raced like it would fly out of her chest, and her body exploded into what felt like a million gloriously sated pieces. Even more awesome, judging by the trembling and panting body curved against her back, Mitchell suffered from it too.

Coming back to her senses, she peered at the clearing only to see the foursome still going at it, not even stopping to take note of the momentous event that just occurred. Mitchell had marked her.

And once she marked him back, they'd belong to each other forever. His wet cock slid from her as he turned her in his arms into a hug that pressed them together, skin to skin.

"I love you, Mitchell," she whispered against his chest, her ear pressed against it, soothed by the erratic beat of his heart.

"I love you too, Red. I just wish it hadn't taken me this long to figure it out."

"So now what?" she asked, glancing up at him, loving how he already gazed down at her with such a soft expression.

"Now, we leave those guys to finish their business and we go find a bed before I forget myself again and take you like an animal."

"But I liked it," she sassed. "A lot."

His chest rumbled with laughter. "As did I. But, I don't need you suffering from a relapse."

"I'm fine."

"Humor me."

"Fine. But only because you bit me. Just so you know, though, I will be biting you back, preferably while riding you cowgirl style."

"It'll have to wait until your place is ready because my family might hear."

"So try and stay quiet."

He groaned. "You are incorrigible."

"Yes, and insatiable," she whispered, leaning up to kiss him.

He only allowed a light embrace before stepping away, his sated cock already trying to rise. "Bad wolf. Come on before I forget my good intentions, again."

"Spoilsport." Shifting into their wolf skins, she took stock of her body as they trotted back. She didn't feel any twinges at all where she'd been shot. Actually, she felt great. And more than ready for another round.

As they made their way back to his house, they heard the howls, yeowls, and other wild sounds signalling others of their kind who'd chosen to roam the wood tonight, enjoying the full moon. It still shocked her that Mitchell had stayed to watch the foursome they'd caught going at it. It seemed Mitchell was a voyeur, the sight of others enjoying erotic pleasures a turn on, which gave her such hope that in the near future, once Alejandro claimed her as well, perhaps they could indulge in something equally naughty.

Even if they took turns, just having him there, watching, getting turned on… Damn, they needed to get back quick or she'd jump his ass again here in the woods, bed or not.

It seemed to take forever for them to reach their piles of clothes, now neatly folded, probably courtesy of his mother. They dressed in silence, although the heated looks fairly screamed. He kept peeking at her as she dressed, the bulge of his cock impossible to ignore. She didn't even pretend. She just stared at him outright and licked her lips. They snuck into the house, the soft sound of the television in the living room letting them know not everyone had left to enjoy the night air. Creeping up the stairs, she fought hard not to giggle. Talk about a flashback to teenage years.

They made it to his room and he shut the door then locked it before turning to face her with glittering eyes. She flopped on the bed and grinned.

"Found the bed. Why are you still wearing clothes?"

Muttering something about bossy woman, smiling as he did, and with an erection that showed it didn't irritate him in the least, he stripped.

She did the same, until she lay on his bed naked, the flames of her arousal already lit. She would have thought their satisfying encounter in the woods would have sated her somewhat, but oddly, she found herself even more frantic for him than before. She yanked him down beside her on the bed, then rolled atop him, straddling his waist.

"Now I've got you where I want you," she whispered.

"Move a little more south and you'll be right where I want you," he said back with a leer.

Dirty talk again from her Mitchell. How awesome. She wiggled her ass against his shaft, which butted against her. She lifted herself and poised herself over the crown of it then looked at him coyly. "Do you mean here?"

"Almost," he said, his voice strained.

She'd torture him later. Right now, she wanted the same thing he did. His cock buried inside of her. She sat down hard, enveloping his prick in a swift motion that saw his hips bucking, and he bit his lips when he would have shouted.

"Shh," she taunted. "We don't want anyone to come checking on us," she whispered.

His eyes glittered and a smile curved his lips as he thrust up into her, gyrating his pelvis enough to rub on her G spot. It was her turn to bite her lip lest she gasp aloud. "You did that on purpose," she hissed.

He just grinned wider. Oh God, just like her, the idea of getting caught made him wild.

Two could have so much fun playing that game. Digging her nails into his pecs, she rode her wild wolf, bouncing up and down on his rigid length, suctioning him tight with her sex. He teased her mercilessly back, the fingers on one hand reaching out to tweak her pointed nipples while the other slid between their bodies and toyed with her clit. Her passion built up fast and furious, a coiling pressure inside that needed relief.

When she feared crying out at the intense beauty of it, she flopped forward, crushing her breasts against his chest and burying her face into the curve of his neck. Still, though, she rocked on him, her bliss building and building until it exploded and she opened her mouth wide on a scream over his skin, but instead of loosing what surely would have been an ear-shattering sound, she bit down.

Mitchell went wild under her, his hips pumping up into her, strangled moans the only sound he dared make as she finally claimed her Mitchell. *My mate, for now and ever.*

Collapsing in a sweaty heaving heap on top of him, she enjoyed the gentle touch of his hands as they rubbed circles on her back. So sated and happy was she in that moment that when Chris shouted, "Are you done making the bed shake? The damn plaster is falling in the living room," she didn't even mind when Mitchell dumped her on the mattress and went tearing out of the bedroom buck naked.

It's official. I'm one of the family.

Chapter Twelve

Francine sensed him before he even had a chance to knock, jumping up from her scrubbing position on her knees to fly to the door. She flung the portal open and threw herself in Alejandro's arms, wrapping her arms around his neck and her legs about his waist.

"Now that's a welcome," he quipped in her ear, squeezing her back just as tight.

"What took you so long?" she asked as he carted her clinging frame into her town house.

"My bike died. I ended up having to wait for my brothers to show up with my car and Ignacio's pickup truck. They took my bike back to see if they can bring it back to life, and I drove back here as fast as I could."

"You should have called," she admonished.

"I, um, kind of got mad when the bike died and might have pitched my phone," he admitted sheepishly.

A giggle escaped her. "Naomi's done that more times than I can count."

"Where's the dog?" he asked, letting her slide down his body, a very nice body that she'd missed.

"Here." Mitchell came out of the kitchen wiping his hands on a dishrag. They'd come over to her place right after breakfast to work on the rest of the cleanup before the new furniture arrived.

Alejandro left her side to stride over to Mitchell…and held out his hand. A wary look on his face, Mitchell shook it. "Congratulations on your mating."

A blush crept up Francine's cheeks. He knew. Was it that obvious? And would it change his intentions toward her? Despite the fact Mitchell would prefer to keep her to himself, she didn't want to give Alejandro up. The very idea made her wolf whine.

"Thank you, I think. You aren't pissed?" Mitchell seemed bemused, and Alejandro grinned.

"It's not about me, but Francine. Besides, I'm sure it's obvious to you by now just how much of a handful she is. It will be nice to have an extra set of hands helping out, not to mention another body to protect her should the need arise."

"You mean like now."

Both men turned to stare at her with grim faces.

"What? It's not my fault Mitchell was dating a psycho. Anyway, with both of you here, I doubt she'll try anything. She lost. I won. End of story."

Judging by the glance they exchanged, they didn't think so. She, however, wouldn't live forever looking over her shoulder. Jenny had freaked and lashed out. She had to know she was in major trouble and with no one able to find her, had probably hightailed it out of the province. Maybe even the country. But, let her mate, and soon-to-be mate worry about it. She kind of enjoyed their bristling, macho protector roles. Her wolf liked it too and thought she should thank them—naked.

What a shame Mitchell had flat out stated no to an actual threesome.

"Have you guys had lunch yet?" Alejandro asked, coming back to her side to slide an arm around her waist for a half hug.

Mitchell shook his head. "No. And there's nothing edible here. Why don't you go to lunch? I've got to go check in with my work. I took the week off to care for Francine and they're probably wondering if I'm ever coming back."

Francine's jaw almost hit the floor, surprised by Mitchell's suggestion. "Are you coming back?"

"I'll bring some Chinese for dinner. That is if the cat here isn't afraid one of his relatives is part of the menu." Mitchell flashed a grin full of teeth that made Alejandro laugh as he shrugged off the implied insult.

"Cats are never averse to eating pussy," he replied.

Francine snorted, then laughed at the look on Mitchell's face. "Oh, this is going to be fun."

Shaking his head, Mitchell strode toward her and pulled her from Alejandro's side. He enveloped her in a hug of his own, dipping his head to kiss her. Kissed her thoroughly, as a matter of fact, with some tongue, some ass grabbing, and some definite groin grinding. When he finally let her up for air, she panted with flushed cheeks—and an even wetter pussy.

"Since he gets you for the afternoon, you're mine tonight," he stated, then he left.

A sigh slipped from her.

"Don't worry, baby. He's just making sure I know he's not going anywhere."

"I'm sorry, though. That was kind of in your face."

"Don't be sorry. I enjoyed it. Watching you get pleasured is highly arousing. And I think your dog enjoys having an audience."

Francine bit her lips so as to not blurt that being watched wasn't the only voyeuristic aspect Mitchell enjoyed. She'd have to tread carefully with him if she was to make things work and keep both her men. But, at least knowing how much Mitchell enjoyed watching gave her hope that one day he'd look past his jealousy of Alejandro and realize—make that experience—the fun the three of them could have together.

And maybe she'd grow wings.

Then again, not so long ago, she'd wondered if she'd ever snag the man she'd loved for so long. It just went to show miracles could and did happen.

"Enough of that pensive face. Let's go eat. I want you fully energized for what I have planned this afternoon."

"And just what do you have planned?"

"Some pasta for lunch, some pie for dessert, and a chunk of heaven to top it all off."

"That all?" she teased.

"Oh, there's the minor matter of claiming the woman I intend to worship for the rest of my life, but I'm sure you don't care about that part."

She slapped him in the arm. "Tease."

"Oh, I intend to be."

And he lived up to his word. All through their lunch, pressed tightly together in their booth, he tormented her; his hand sliding up her thigh to brush the apex of legs, whispering in her ear, his lips and teeth tugging at her earlobe, everything coming out as an innuendo. She paid him back in kind, though, slipping her own hand under the table to massage his cock through his jeans to his softly groaned enjoyment, teasing him with her own erotic implications until they both just about tore their clothes off, so fiercely did their desire burn.

Excusing herself from the table to go to the washroom, she told herself that she needed a moment to compose herself before they left, but really what she wanted was to wipe the sauce off her shirt before Alejandro gave a show to the whole restaurant sucking it off. Damn, but she would have probably enjoyed that.

Looking into the mirror, she couldn't believe her appearance. Eyes bright, cheeks flushed, her lips swollen and red from kisses, she appeared a woman in lust—and so totally in love. Odd how she could so easily admit that to herself now, and not just for one man, but two. Mitchell, with his staid ways but simmering passion whom she adored for so long because of his fierce, protective love for his family and friends. And Alejandro with his light-hearted humor, smoldering eroticism, and way of putting her at ease.

She knew what would happen when they got back to her place. Not cleaning, that was for sure, unless his tongue on her pussy lapping at her honey counted. But beyond the sex, she would claim him, and he would claim her. They'd tie themselves together, a love triangle with her as the connecting point. She only hoped she could make it work and keep them both happy.

Wandering back to the table, and her sensual cat, her steps slowed as she saw a pair of women surrounding Alejandro. The interest in their eyes and the tilt of their bodies let her see their blatant interest in her man. Even worse, they were freakn' gorgeous. Tall, lean with cascading blonde hair and curves that made her feel fat in comparison.

I can't compare with them. A part of her knew she was letting jealousy and insecurity dig its claws in, but seriously, even that knowledge couldn't change the fact Francine would never have that type of model looks. Could she let Alejandro bind himself to her forever knowing she'd probably get even chubbier after they had babies? Would he even want her? How could she…

Turning abruptly, not even excusing himself to the chattering women, he smiled at her, and only her, his eyes lighting up. He held out his hand. "There you are, baby. Are you ready to go home?"

Was she? He never even spared the other women a glance when they strutted off in a huff. The expression in his gaze screamed, "Trust me." She remembered something her grandmother once said, and it had struck her odd at the time but now made so much sense; "Love is taking a leap of faith."

And oh, how she loved the man before her. She extended her hand and he clasped it, drawing her into him.

As if he'd read her doubts and insecurities, he murmured, "No one can compare to you, baby. Let me show you."

She nodded her head and let him lead her from the restaurant. They climbed into his car, a boring four door Intrepid, so unlike his persona, that she had to ask him, "Why the grown up sedan?"

"Big backseat."

His words penetrated and she slapped his arm, jealousy making her speak without curbing her tongue. "You'd better get it steam cleaned."

"What?" He peered over at her, saw her lips set in a mulish line, and laughed. "You thought I— Never mind, it's obvious what you thought, but that's actually not what I meant. Until you, I never liked sleeping with a woman and sometimes I was a little too tipsy to drive. So, the big back seat doubled great as a bed for the times I need to sleep one off before driving home."

"Oh."

"Ha. I've rendered her speechless and I didn't even have to put something in your mouth to do it."

"Thought about ways to gag me, have you?"

"The entire time I was gone," he admitted with no shame.

"I'd hate for you to go on wondering," she replied saucily. The desire she'd kept under control through lunch, since the moment he'd returned actually, took over. She wanted Alejandro, needed him. Needed to feel his touch. Needed his love. *Need to claim,* her wolf added pacing her mind, impatient to make this man theirs.

Leaning over, she unzipped his pants, her hand delving in the opening to stroke his semi-hard cock through his briefs.

"This is probably a stupid question, but what are you doing, baby?"

"I am going to blow you," she stated calmly, bending over further until her face hovered over his lap. Commuters in other vehicles didn't matter—let them watch. The fact he drove and they courted danger couldn't stop her—they'd heal. The raging fire inside her demanded action, and she obeyed.

"But the traffic… Aren't you…Aaahh." He ended his feeble protests on a sigh as she pulled him free and sucked him into her mouth. Up and down, she worked his shaft, her lips pulled taut over his girth, her teeth lightly grazing his skin. The more she suctioned, the more his cock hardened, the fat vein on the underside pulsing erratically against her tongue. Oh to taste his essence, to make him lose control.

Faster and faster, she bobbed, only vaguely noticing the car stopped. Impatient hands pulled her up. Alejandro's lips found hers and latched on for a scorching kiss. The same urgency that imbued her came through in his embrace. His lips slid over hers, devouring, sucking, tasting, his tongue melding with hers until she didn't know where one began and the other stopped.

That wasn't all he did, though. His hand crept up her thigh, rubbing against her core through the fabric of her slacks, making her moan against his mouth. Wet, so fucking wet.

Heart pounding madly, sex throbbing deliciously, she could only moan incoherently, straining against the hand that stroked her, begging for a more intimate touch.

Sensing her need for more, he unbuttoned her pants and slid his hand in. Fingers slid through her curls to find her clit and rub it. She gasped against his mouth, her hips jerking as her body reacted to his caress.

"Aren't you supposed to be driving?" she panted, wondering with a distant humor if they were stopped in traffic with an audience. How exciting.

"I found us a parking garage."

"A what?" She allowed herself a quick glance around, noting they were in a fluorescent lighted area, with cars parked all around them.

"I need you, Francine." He said the words in a rough voice, his urgency clear in his eyes and tone.

"Then let's put that back seat of yours to good use." She managed to squeeze between the front seats into the back, but when he would have followed, his bigger frame got caught. She couldn't help the husky giggle as he cursed and squirmed, unable to fit himself through the small space.

And of course she didn't help matters. Cupping her breasts, she stroked her thumbs over erect peaks that strained against the fabric of her top. "Hurry, Jag. Hurry and get back here before I take care of myself." She coasted a hand down her body and slid her hand into the opening of her pants, right into her panties and cupped her moist sex. She moaned, not just at the heat of her pussy, but the wild light in his eyes.

In a flash, he'd pulled himself out of the wedge between the front seats and got out of the car. Opening the rear passenger door, he hesitated before entering. With his pants already undone and his cock straining through the opening, he was the picture of male out of control. And she'd done that. What a heady feeling.

He pushed his jeans down around his knees before clambering in. Francine, already sprawled lengthwise on the seat, held her arms out for him. He fell on her, his mouth hungry for a kiss, his hands impatiently yanking at her slacks, tearing them the rest of the way down.

The windows steamed up as they embraced and stroked, frantic in their need, desperate to reach that blissful peak.

"Now, Jag, I need you." She hiked a leg up, looping her calf over the driver seat, spreading herself for him. He wasted no time, driving his cock into her moist core, his hard thrust filling her up so deliciously and satisfying the part of her that had missed him so much.

"Oh fuck, baby. I need you so freakn' much," he growled as he pumped. "Those days without you were pure torture," he panted as he claimed her with his cock.

Her fingers dug into his back as she arched into his thrusts, her own desire just as great. "I love you, Jag, so much it almost hurts. I want you forever." Would die without him in her life. Hell, she'd probably expire if she didn't cum soon as well.

"I'm already yours," he whispered, burying his face into her neck. "And now the world will know it too." With those words, he bit her, his incisors sinking into her flesh, marking her, claiming her as his. *His woman. His mate.*

Francine screamed as the sense of connection, the rightness of his act roared through her, triggering her climax. Her body heaved and convulsed around and against his, but she didn't lose sight of the important thing she had to do. *Make him ours,* her wolf whispered.

"My turn," she murmured. Alejandro released her skin, but not before giving her new mark a lick. Still pumping into her, his cock pulsed, and she felt the tension in his neck against her lips as he fought to hold on. She shattered his control to hell when she bit him back. *Now, you belong to me.*

With a roar, he came inside her, murmuring her name over and over. "Francine, Francine, fuck, how I love you."

Not exactly Shakespearean poetry, but still a beautiful declaration she'd treasure forever.

And it would, of course, happen in the backseat of a car.

Chapter Thirteen

Alejandro couldn't stop grinning. He'd bound himself to one woman for life, and by damn, he'd never felt happier. He held Francine's hand all the way home. People talked about mating and the fever. They made it sound like some big deal. How right they were, and wrong because it transcended big deal into freakn' awesome and unbelievable, yet so perfectly right.

Of course, he wished he'd chosen a more romantic locale to claim his mate—the back seat of his car in an underground garage not exactly his first place choice—but still, it was the end result that mattered. *I am mated.*

Sure, he knew that the mating itself only covered a part of it. The bigger task now remained in making his claim, along with Mitchell's, work in harmony lest they upset Francine. For his part, he didn't foresee a problem. His openness about sexuality meant he could accept different forms of sexual pleasure. While sharing had never before been high on his list of things to do—unless it involved two women—now that he found himself in the position where he had to share with another man, he didn't find himself as averse to it as he would have thought. Seeing Mitchell kissing Francine earlier didn't trigger jealousy. Arousal, yes, but no urge to thump the other male into submission. Would he feel the same way if he came across Mitchell sinking his cock into Francine?

Judging by his hardening shaft, he'd enjoy that visual stimulation. He also knew from small hints that Francine wouldn't mind it as well, but how to bring Mitchell on board?

He pondered that dilemma as they showered together, making love slowly on her new king-sized mattress. He turned the problem over in his mind as he helped Francine finish cleaning up and rearranging the new furniture when it arrived. He'd not come up with a solution once Mitchell arrived with dinner.

Without even sparing him a glance, the wolf swept Francine into his arms and kissed her, surely smelling and tasting Alejandro on her and seeming determined to mask that fact with his own scent. Alejandro fought a grin as he took the bags with the Chinese dinner and pulled out the cartons to set them on the breakfast counter.

"Well hello to you too," he finally heard Francine say when Mitchell let her up for air.

"I wasn't sure what you'd enjoy, so I brought a little of everything. I assume the cat is staying for dinner?"

"Yes, I am, just like I'm sleeping here tonight."

Mitchell froze in the process of grabbing utensils. "But you had her this afternoon. I thought tonight would be my turn."

"Okay, hold on. Before you both turn my nicely cleaned house into a war zone, Mitchell, Jag has to stay here, he's got nowhere else to go, and as my mate, his place is with me." Before Mitchell could protest, she held up her hand. "Just like as my other mate, you should stay here too, if you want. As to the whole taking turns thing, what are the chances of you both working on it amicably?"

Alejandro grinned. "I'm easy."

"So the whole world has heard," Mitchell replied snarkily.

"Care to see me in action and find out what the buzz is about? Maybe you'll learn something," he replied, unable to help himself. Mitchell's nostrils flared, but it wasn't entirely in anger. Interest smoldered for a moment there too.

"Pervert. I agreed to this three-way only because Francine wanted it. As far as I'm concerned, you could fuck off."

"I get better results when I fuck on, or in."

"Do you ever take anything seriously?"

"Yes, Francine's happiness, which I might add, you're fucking with. Leave the jealousy at the door."

"I'm in perfect control, but that doesn't mean I'm not going to make sure I get my fair share of time with her. Just because you've already moved in doesn't mean you should get more of her time."

Francine waved her hand between them. "Um, hello. Living, breathing object of discussion sitting right here. Mitchell, are you saying you're going to be staying at your parents still?"

"What else do you expect me to do? I'm not sharing a bed with the cat even if you're in it."

"But it's a king-size," Alejandro quipped. "More than enough room."

Mitchell glared at him.

"Listen, what if I moved my office and scrapbooking crap from the spare room and made it into a second bedroom? Then on the nights I spend with Jag, you can still be here so I can see you in the morning."

Mitchell didn't say anything for a moment, and Alejandro wanted to punch him as Francine's face fell.

His jaw tense, Mitchell finally nodded in agreement. "Fine. We'll see how that works. But if you don't mind, I'd like for us to look for a bigger house. Somewhere we won't be on top of each other all the time."

Reaching out a hand, Francine covered Mitchell's. "We'll make this work," she said softly.

A vow Alejandro silently repeated to himself. No matter what Mitchell did or said, he'd have to keep his cool. Francine already looked torn at the situation, an unneeded stress caused by Mitchell, who couldn't handle his jealousy.

He'd better get over it or I just might have to beat the little green monster out of him. Or…tempt him by tying the bastard up and making love to Francine in front of him until he's overcome with desire and forgets all about his foolish notions of not sharing.

He liked the second option a lot as a matter of fact.

* * * *

Despite Mitchell's ornery nature, they slipped into a routine, a scheduled one that made Alejandro want to bang his head off a wall.

Mondays, Wednesdays and Fridays, he got to sleep—very little—with his darling Francine. Mitchell got Tuesdays, Wednesday and Saturday nights, with the weekend daytime spent doing together activities like laundry, housework, or hiking. Sundays were Francine's day of rest and as an added maddening bonus, included family dinner with Mitchell's family. The only saving grace was watching the family dynamics at work.

Alejandro revised his earlier opinion that his family was more chaotic. One food fight at Mitchell's parent's house, taught him otherwise.

With them working during the day, and only meeting up at dinner, they spent the hours during the week before bedtime conversing, not as stiffly as in the beginning, especially once Mitchell realized Alejandro was a sports fanatic. Of course, it took the dog some soft pleadings on Francine's part to accept her sitting between them on the couch when they watched television. Alejandro knew he should not antagonize the fragile peace during these moments of truce, but whenever Mitchell got up to get them a beer or hit the bathroom, he had a tendency of making sure to have his tongue meshed with Francine's before the dog came back. Mitchell never said a word when that happened, although his jaw would tighten and he'd sit stiffly for a bit. Until Alejandro left the room that was, then he'd come back to find the wolf all over Francine, rubbing his scent into her, flashing him a triumphant smile that made their mate shake her head.

"Like a fucking chew toy," she'd mutter. But so long as they didn't come to physical blows, she let them handle their marking of territory their way. Alejandro found the situation kind of amusing, especially since he knew Mitchell enjoyed watching him with Francine, and while he'd spent a few nights at his parents the first week of their arrangement, he now stayed home the nights Alejandro made Francine scream in passion. And if he were to guess, Mitchell did the same thing Alejandro did when he heard the moaning start. Got the lube out of the drawer and fisted himself.

But he knew things couldn't go on the way they were. This clear division of territory wore on poor Francine, although she never said a word of protest, unwilling to rock the tentative boat.

Things came to a head about a month after they claimed her, and at the Sunday family dinner of all things.

Chris, the family fight instigator, finally lit the match that caused the situation to explode.

"Hey brother, what's this I hear about you keeping a separate bedroom? Afraid Jag's cock will put yours to shame?"

Already tense, because Sundays was the day all of them slept alone because of Mitchell, the wolf snapped and dove over the table at his brother. While they rolled around the floor, trading blows, their mother ignoring them as she cleared the table for dessert, Alejandro looked over to Francine and saw her sniffing back tears.

"Baby, what's wrong?" he asked, immediately concerned.

"Nothing," she cried before jumping up to run from the table.

Moving to follow, he found himself restrained and looked down to see Naomi's hand on his arm, her nails digging into his arm. "Sit down."

"But Francine—"

"Will be fine for a minute. Ethan, grab my brother, will you? The stupid one, not the ugly one."

Her bear shrugged and swooped down to grab a still swinging Mitchell. With a snarl, the wolf righted himself and glared at his sister. "What?"

"Are you done being an idiot? Can't you see you're making Francine miserable?"

"What are you talking a—" Mitchell looked around, and not finding their mate, concern blossomed.

"She's gone off to cry. Again."

"What do you mean again?" Mitchell whispered sitting down hard. "I haven't seen her crying."

"Okay, so this is only the second time that I know of. Still, it's two times too many, and it's all your fault."

"Me? Why is it my fault? Why not blame that stupid cat over there? He's her mate too, you know?"

"He is, and I know for a fact he's not the one acting like a jealous ass all the time. Can't you see that your insistence not to share her and to make her choose between you constantly is hurting her? Do you care so little for her that you would let your ego hurt the one person who doesn't deserve it?"

"She's right." Mitchell's mother agreed, coming in with two cakes—vanilla and chocolate. "You never did share well with others. I was hoping that would change with both your animals choosing her as mate, but I guess there's a first time for fate to be wrong."

"Francine's my mate." Mitchell almost shouted the claim.

"And mine too."

"So you say, and yet, you're both here while she's off crying."

"You stopped me from going after her," Alejandro corrected.

"Yes, I did because it's not one of you at a time she needs. It's both of you. So, are you going to smarten up and do right by her, or am I going to have to—Oooh."

"Naomi?" Javier jumped up from his seat and hovered over her.

"I think—Ow! Dammit, I wasn't done talking, but it seems the babies are coming."

Alejandro quite enjoyed the panic in brother's eyes, almost as much as the white faced-shock of Ethan.

"Call a doctor. Boil some water," Javier yelled.

Ethan scooped her up and growled at people to get out of his way while Naomi giggled. "I'm going into labor, not dying. Mama, would you tell them to not panic?"

"But it's our first child," Javier said, standing shoulder to shoulder with Ethan.

"Yes, but we're a team. Remember, no matter what, we're going to do this together. I love you, and now get ready because we're about to make that love grow." Ethan and Javier gazed into their mate's face with such love that Alejandro had to look away, feeling as if he encroached on something personal, something special. *The very thing Francine longs for.*

Flicking a glance over at Mitchell, he caught him just turning away as well. As their eyes met, Alejandro saw understanding lighten his eyes, followed by resolve. "If you'll excuse us, Alejandro and I need to find Francine and let her know."

As they left the room, following Francine's trace outside and wandering into the woods, Mitchell said only one thing as he stripped and left his clothes atop Francine's already discarded ones. "Let's go give our mate what she needs."

How ironic, that what their mate needed was a good bout of loving with both of her men at once. All couples should have such a solution to their marital problems.

Chapter Fourteen

Francine didn't know why she took off, tears streaming down her face. Mitchell getting upset over someone mentioning their odd living arrangement happened more often than she liked. And she liked it less and less. The longer the situation went on, with her belonging to two men but forced to keep them apart, the more she felt like a game ball getting tossed between her mates. Tired of it, she wanted escape, even if for a little while, run away and forget her problems. So she did, stripping naked in the yard and letting her bitch loose.

Stretching her legs, running through the woods, the crisp autumn air cleansing, she raced to forget her woes. But they dragged along inside her.

How can having what I wanted make me so unhappy? That wasn't quite accurate. She was happy, most of the time. The hurt came from having to constantly watch her actions around Mitchell. To have to say goodnight to one of her mates every night when all she wanted was to sleep between them. The problem had nothing to do with sex, even if she could so easily imagine it—naked and undulating between her two mate's bodies. The problem arose from feeling like she carried on two separate relationships when all she wanted was one seamless one, a polyamorous love like Naomi had. Her BFF didn't worry about giving one mate too much affection, or whose turn it was to fuck, or who would sleep where. They lived, screwed, and loved as one. *Lucky freakn' bitch.*

The worst part? She knew Alejandro would give it to her in an instant. She'd even seen his attempts to tempt and goad Mitchell into becoming a true threesome. Sometimes, he almost succeeded like when they hiked, or went to watch a hockey game and booed together. But as soon as nine o'clock hit, Mitchell would drag her off with barely a good night to her cat, or on his off nights, he'd skulk off and closet himself in the spare room. It broke her heart each time.

But I knew this when I chose him. Mitchell never hid the fact his jealousy wouldn't let him share.

So, now she needed to suck it up, pull up her princess panties, and stop whining like that loser bitch Jenny. Just thinking about the anorexic slut cheered her up. Word through the grapevine was she'd fled out west to visit her aunt rather than face the consequences of her actions. She never made it, though, getting claimed halfway through the prairies by a buffalo shifter. Even funnier, Jenny's new mate lived on a farm smack dab in the middle of the plains, without a mall in sight. The crowning touch? The man was short and built like a keg. Francine loved it when karma bit people on the ass and she couldn't think of a nicer person for karma to have fucked with.

Maybe I'll send her a Christmas card and thank her for shooting me because it is, after all, what made Mitchell finally realize he loved me. Now if only some other psycho bitch would come crawling out of the woodwork and convince Mitchell to stop acting like a jealous ass. Somehow, she doubted she'd get that lucky twice.

Flopping to the ground, in the clearing where she and Mitchell had watched that foursome the night of her claiming, she shifted back to her human shape. She rolled onto her back and stared up at the sky, the stars just beginning to twinkle.

Lost in her thoughts, she didn't hear the creature approach, and her inner wolf didn't bother to warn her, having recognized the scent. A large, furry, black head rubbed itself on her belly, Alejandro wearing his kitty. Her fingers stroked the fur behind his ears and she giggled as he purred, the loud rumble vibrating against her skin.

"Sorry I ran off," she murmured.

"And I'm sorry I made you run away," Mitchell said as he strode from the darkness, the soft glow of the quarter moon making his skin glint. The fur-covered head on her belly shifted as Alejandro retook his man shape and Francine tensed as she waited for Mitchell to turn and walk away. Or engage her cat in a fight of words, or would they finally come to fists? It wouldn't be the first time, although they usually never did it when she was around.

To her shock, Mitchell dropped to her other side and laid his head against her as well, the dark hairs of her mates actually touching. Unwilling to breathe or say anything to break this miracle, she held herself still.

"I know I've made things hard," Mitchell said. To his credit, Alejandro didn't say anything inflammatory. "I wish I could say it was jealousy or dislike that made me do and say the things I've done."

"It's not jealousy?" She couldn't help the surprised lilt in her query.

"Yes and no. Yes, a part of me wants to be the only one you touch and to not share any part of your body, smile or love. But, another part of me wants to see you with Jag, to watch as he fucks you, and even…" He stopped.

"Join in?"

A loud sigh left him. "Yes. It seems so wrong. I mean. My dad only has my mom. And all my buddies, those that mated anyway, only ended up with one girl. Admitting I want to be with you and another guy at the same time just seems so… I don't know, perverted."

"I prefer dirty. And hot. Oh, and so arousing," she murmured, allowing her hand to finally drift up and sift through the two tousled heads on her bare stomach.

"I don't want him touching me," Mitchell growled.

"Why would he do that when you're both going to be too busy pleasuring me? I am, after all, the one who needs two men."

"Then I guess it's time I stopped acting like a pussy here, and gave you what you wanted." Mitchell turned his head, his dark eyes staring into hers, and he smiled, a sweet smile of surrender, and of acceptance. Finally. "So how does this work then?"

Alejandro spoke for her. "Now, we show our mate what ecstasy can be found when two mouths and hands touch her at the same time."

"Finally, the cat says something I like," Mitchell replied, his voice thick with desire. Then, her mates proceeded to show instead of just tell.

They lifted themselves onto their hands and knees, their mouths hovering over her aching peaks. At almost the same instant, they latched on, their hot mouths tugging at her nipples, similar and yet so different, the sensation making her arch against them.

Hands roamed her body, stroking her flesh, squeezing her breasts, teasing the moist lips between her thighs. Light, tickling touches that had her arching and mewling for more. Then demanding.

"Stop teasing me," she growled.

"What do you want?" her cat purred, rubbing his face against her lower stomach.

"Lick me, then fuck me while I suck." Crude words that nevertheless had both her mates groaning.

"She's trying to kill us."

"It's a good thing there's two of us to take care of Red's needs. Will you do the honor of taking care of her sweet pussy while I shut her up?"

Her eyes widened as suddenly in cahoots, they took charge of the situation, flipping her onto her stomach, then pulling her up onto her hands and knees. Fingers gripped her hair and guided her mouth to the bobbing cock in front of her. Like she needed help doing what she'd asked for.

She took Mitchell's thick cock into her mouth, sucking at the silky skin with enthusiasm as behind her, Alejandro parted her thighs and his fingers tickled her cleft.

"Fuck, Red, I'm going to have to videotape this for you. You should see it, how he's touching that sweet pussy of yours. Spreading you open." Mitchell gave her a byplay of the action, his voice thick with arousal.

"Mmm, a camera. I'll add it to the shopping list," Alejandro said before touching his mouth to the spot his fingers had just stroked. She keened around the cock in her mouth, causing Mitchell to grunt and thrust forward.

Through gritted teeth, he said, "Oh yeah, Red. Suck my dick while I watch your sweet little pussy getting eaten. He's got his tanned hands on your white ass, spreading you wide. I almost wish I was beside him so I could see him tongue fucking you."

She moaned, almost painfully aroused not only by their actions, but Mitchell's oh so naughty words. It seemed when he'd given himself permission to finally indulge in his taboo fantasy, he'd let loose of the inhibitions that held his tongue. How incredibly pleasurable.

A loud groan emerged from Mitchell as she inhaled him, harder and faster, his hips pumping in time to her mouth.

"I think she's ready," Mitchell panted. "Fuck her. I want to watch."

"My pleasure," purred Alejandro, and then he slammed himself home.

* * * *

Talk about erotic overload. Mitchell just about shot his cream into Francine's mouth when he saw Alejandro's long, smooth prick thrust into her. He knew she enjoyed it from the way her mouth went slack around him as she lost focus, to the visual evidence in her shaking body that rocked back against the cock slamming her.

The jealousy he'd once feared didn't surface. Instead, he found himself riveted and part of the action, as excited watching her getting pumped as if he'd slid into her himself. He could no longer form coherent sentences or he would have told Francine how beautiful he found it. How arousing. Letting his cock slip from her slack mouth, he moved to the side, unable to stop himself from taking a closer look, his hand stroking his dick as he watched.

"She has such a responsive little body," Jag said in between grunts and thrusts. "See how she takes me and begs for more? Touch her underneath. Stroke her little nub and you'll see how she quivers."

Doing as Alejandro said, Mitchell's free hand moved under and slid through her curls to her slippery nub. He almost snatched his hand away when he inadvertently touched the cat's dick as it slid in, but fascination brought his finger back to circle and rub her clit. Francine screamed and Mitchell fisted himself faster as he saw her buttocks clench and her sex suck Alejandro's prick into its tight grip.

"Yes, baby. Yes!" Alejandro threw his head back as he humped himself deep into her, his fingers digging into her fleshy ass cheeks as he found his pleasure.

It was fucking amazing. *And to think I denied myself this pleasure for the last month.* How stupid he felt now, especially knowing his love of watching—and as he discovered, even listening. How often had he jerked off listening to their lovemaking, wishing he had the nerve to join, wondering if he could handle it? Fisting his cock faster, he knew the answer.

"Your turn," the cat said, interrupting his thoughts and drawing his attention away from her shuddering body.

"But—" Surely, she needed time to recover, but Mitchell didn't protest as Alejandro pushed him down, Francine's smaller hands aiding him, her brown eyes regarding him with…hunger. Despite her screaming orgasm, it seemed his woman wasn't yet done. She licked her lips as she straddled him.

"Wait," Jag said. "Turn around and sit on him this way. I have a treat for you. Mitchell, sit up and hold her against your chest."

Curious, and still hard as a rock, Mitchell sat up, his cock jutting from his groin and straining toward Francine's core, which hovered over him. Alejandro didn't touch him, but he still managed to guide her onto his dick, her velvety heat squeezing around him, the faint tremors of her climax aftershocks sending tingles through his shaft.

Remembering Alejandro's instructions, he wrapped his arm around her waist while the other braced itself on the ground behind. He thrust up into her, and his delightful Red pushed back, sinking herself deep onto his cock. But while she sighed in pleasure, he could tell she was far from coming again, or at least much farther than him as he pretty much sat on the brink.

"Lean back a bit more," Alejandro whispered, his soft breath somehow tickling his balls.

Alarmed, Mitchell peered over her shoulder, only to groan as he saw the cat flick out his tongue and dart it against her exposed clit. A shudder went through her. Alejandro lapped at her again. Another tremor. Each time he licked, she shook, the muscles of her pussy spasming, fisting him tight. It was fucking amazing.

Worry that the cat strayed too close to his man parts dissipated as Mitchell lost himself to the mounting pleasure, a pleasure increased as Alejandro's actions brought Francine back up to that hill of pleasure, and with deft strokes of his tongue, pushed her over so that she screamed once again in climax, milking his shaft and making him bellow as he came at last inside her.

Blown away, chest heaving, and sweaty even in the autumn air, they collapsed, he and Jag somehow ending up side by side with her sprawled across them.

"That was unfreakn' believable," she groaned. "I think I might have died and gone to heaven. No, wait. I hope not, because I really want to do that again."

214

"Insatiable brat," Alejandro chuckled.

"I'm lusty, so sue me," she sassed. "What about you, Mitchell, did you enjoy it?"

Concerned brown eyes peered at him, and he almost laughed in disbelief. Had she not noticed how hard he'd come? "I don't know. I think we'll need to try it again, say maybe a few thousand times, then I'll let you know. Of course I enjoyed it and before you say I told you so, I already know I'm a dumbass for fighting it for so long."

She leaned up to kiss him lightly. "Never dumb. Just unsure. I love you so much, Mitchell. Thanks for giving this to me."

"No, thank you."

"Why don't we all thank each other by going for a swim in the stream and seeing if we can re-create the magic?"

The water turned out too cold, but it didn't stop the giggles and laughter as they splashed each other and chased Francine around until they noted her teeth chattering.

Slapping her on the ass, he realized something. He and Alejandro were her mates and for more than just sex. They were also partners when it came to taking care of Francine, a beautiful woman whom they both dearly loved. And despite himself, much as it pained him to admit, he liked the damned cat. There were worse people he could have gotten stuck with for a lifetime. Besides, at least the man knew how to play lacrosse against Javier and Ethan. Not to mention, he knew some interesting bedroom techniques that he looked forward to learning, and most of all, applying first hand.

Of course, mentally admitting these things to himself didn't mean he'd tell the cat he liked him. He enjoyed their verbal sparring too much, but when it came to sharing Francine, though, he was done fighting. Her happiness was the only thing that truly mattered to him, and what luck, her version of happiness meant incredible pleasure.

* * * *

Sated and grinning like idiots, they finally stumbled back into the house to the shrieking of an angry she-wolf.

"You bastards! You planted these basketballs inside me. I am going rip your dicks off. Ooooh!"

Francine turned wide eyes to her mates who shrugged sheepishly.

Mitchell turned red. "Um, in the heat of the moment, did we forget to mention Naomi went into labor?"

And that was the last coherent thing anybody said for a while as the family took turns holding Naomi's hand, enduring her punishing grip when she freaked and demanded her men leave. Not that Ethan or Javier went far. They paced the hallway, their faces tight with anxiety, but not willing to miss the birth of their children no matter how pissed their delicate freakn' flower was at the moment.

During one of her periods with her BFF, as Francine mopped her brow, Naomi stopped groaning long enough to say, "So, tell me. Was it good?"

A smile curved her lips as she sassed back, "Oh please, like you didn't hear me screaming over your pissing and moaning."

"Skank."

"Bitch."

They grinned at each other for a moment before another contraction hit and Naomi went back to cursing mankind. The laboring went on for a few more hours, with the same doctor who'd tended Francine arriving to supervise the birth. Just after midnight, Mark and Melanie were born at a screaming five pounds four ounces, and four pounds eleven.

They were red, wrinkly, and possessed the mightiest pair of lungs ever seen. In other words, they were adorable and judging by the beatific smiles on Naomi's and the fathers' faces, they agreed. Her men, on the other hand, appeared quite green. The deed done, they wasted no time saying good-bye and leaving the new family alone, dragging her to the car.

On the drive back, not much was said, Francine dozing on and off on Mitchell's lap as Alejandro drove. Once they got to the house, they carried her straight upstairs, two pairs of deft hands stripping her. Then she tensed as she waited to see if they'd leave since it was technically Sunday night, or if they'd fight over who got to stay. She smiled as she felt the bed dip on either side of her, two warm and very naked bodies cuddling into her on either side.

"Thank you," she whispered.

"I'm done being jealous and freakn'," Mitchell murmured. "From now on, you're stuck with the both of us. I love you, Red."

"Almost much as I love you, baby."

Lucky me.

Epilogue

Francine and her mates moved into a four bedroom home on a ravine lot nestled in a new subdivision on the outskirts of town that shifters were snatching up due to its prime location next to some protected woodlands.

Domestic life agreed with Francine, especially now that her men had finally learned to share. Although not without the occasional tussle that she ended with a softly spoken, "I'll masturbate tonight if you don't behave." Talk about instant attitude adjustment.

And Naomi was so right about the two-man thing. Two is so much more convenient than one. Take now, for instance. Both her men panted, the sweat glistening off their bare chests as they took turns pleasing her.

"That's it, Mitchell," she crooned. "A little harder. Swirl it. Ooh, yes, almost there, push it now."

"You're going to kill me, Red," he groaned. "Isn't it the cat's turn?"

Alejandro laughed. "Not yet. Come on, you mangy dog, give the woman what she wants. Put your back into it and dig."

With a mighty groan, Mitchell heaved the trunk out of the ground and stumbled back with it.

"You did it," Francine squealed, clapping her hands. And about time too. She'd had them working to get that stump out of the ground for over an hour now, taking turns working at it.

"Glad to serve," huffed Mitchell, sitting down hard on the grass.

"Beer?" Alejandro offered as he stood.

"Not yet, Jag," she said wagging a finger. "You still need to fill that hole. And when you're done, I know another hole that needs filling, after you both shower, of course." She wrinkled her nose, then squealed, as her men, suddenly in cahoots, came after her, wrapping her in a sweaty body hug that would have been more enjoyable if it were erotically induced and naked.

Pleased with themselves, they wandered off to the pile of dirt, and together, filled the wheelbarrow up and wheeled it over to the hole to backfill it. It made her heart swell to see the two of them getting along, even if oftentimes their cooperation involved harassing her. And she absolutely loved it when they tag teamed her in the bedroom.

Lucky her, she now had two men she could count on, and while it started out with one of them jealous and freakn', it turned into a whole lot of love—and sex. Lots of yummy, toe-tingling sex. *I am so freakn' lucky.*

* * * * *

Up the street...

Chris, Naomi's brother, parked at the curb and swung out of his truck. He ambled his way to the back of his work vehicle and pulled the squealing tailgate down so he could heft his toolbox out. Called out on a service call, he tried not to sigh, thinking of the lacrosse game he'd probably miss out on tonight because of this last minute job. *What's the point of having brothers-in-law who give me free tickets if I can't use them?*

Maybe he'd get done quicker than expected. After all, the neighborhood was brand spanking new. How much work could there be?

Knocking on the door, he bounced on the balls of his feet, surveying the neighborhood still under construction. He remembered it from Francine's house warming party a few weeks back. God, the fun he'd had bugging the hell out of Mitchell when on the tour of the house, he'd caught sight of the king-size bed. The broken nose was well worth the ruddy-cheeked embarrassment on his big brother's face, though.

What bad luck, though, Mitchell had to share his woman. Not that Chris disliked Jag. On the contrary, he found Javier's brother highly entertaining, especially since he also excelled at driving Mitchell nuts. But still, while the threesome thing sounded kind of kinky, Chris wasn't the type to want to share, especially not his mate and for life. No way, not him. Besides, with two polyamorous pairings in the family, chances were good they'd hit their quota and hopefully, fate would hold off a few years before introducing him to his lucky lady wolf. He still had quite a few oats he wanted to sow.

The clicking of tumblers as locks disengaged told him someone finally answered the door. He didn't immediately turn, not wanting to appear too eager beaver or in their face.

The smell hit him first. Flowers of some sort with a hint of animal, something exotic that he'd never scented before, mixed in with the musk of a woman. Toe-curling, cock-hardening woman.

Whirling, Chris gaped at the petite female in the doorway. His mate. Or so his yipping wolf seemed to think. Not even reaching his chin, she appeared of Asian background, with dark, slanted eyes, high cheekbones, black hair twined atop her head in bun, and rosebud lips that rounded into an 'O' of surprise.

"Who are you?" he asked, inhaling her scent, and fighting an urge to gather her in his arms and taste her mouth.

"Taken," growled a male sporting the same Asian complexion as he came up behind her and placed his hand on her shoulder possessively.

Ah, freakn' hell. This would make things complicated.

Stay tuned for Chris's story, *Already Freakn' Mated*, coming in 2012.

The End

Author Biography

So you want to know a little about me? Well, I'm in my later thirties, married eleven years to a wonderful, supportive man—yes, he's a hunk—who gave me three beautiful, noisy children aged ten, seven, and five. I work as a webmistress and customer service rep from home, and in my spare time—of which there is tragically too little—I write, read, or Wii.

I was born in British Columbia, but being a military brat lived a little bit everywhere—Quebec, New Brunswick, Labrador, Virginia (USA), and finally Ontario. My family and I currently reside in a historic town just outside of Toronto.

Wow, was that ever boring! Now for the fun stuff.

I'm writing fantasy the way I like it—hot with a touch of fantasy. I enjoy writing stories that blur the boundaries between good and evil, and in some cases stomp all over that fine line. I tend to have a lot of sexual tension in my tales as I think all torrid love affairs start with a tingle in our tummies. My heroes are very male; you could even say borderline chest thumping at times, but they all have one thing in common; an everlasting love and devotion to the one they love.

Visit me on the Web for news on current and upcoming releases at http://www.EveLanglais.com

Thanks for reading. ☺

More Books by Eve Langlais

Published by Amira Press:
Alien Mate
Alien Mate 2
Alien Mate 3
Broomstick Breakdown
Dating Cupid
Pack Series:
Book 1: Defying Pack Law, Book 2: Betraying The Pack
Taming Her Wolf (coming January 16th, 2012)
His Teddy Bear
Scared of Spiders
The Hunter (Realm series)

Published by Liquid Silver Books:
Princess of Hell Series:
Lucifer's Daughter, Snowballs In Hell, Hell's Revenge
Crazy
Date With Death
Hybrid Misfit
Last Minion Standing
Toxic
Wickedest Witch

Published by Cobblestone Press:
A Ghostly Ménage
Apocalypse Cowboy
Cleopatra's Men
Fire and Ice
My Secretary Series (BDSM shorts)

Published by Champagne Books:
Chance's Game (Realm series)
Take A Chance (Realm series)

Published by Eve Langlais
The Geek Job
Bunny And The Bear
Delicate Freakn' Flower
Accidental Abduction
Intentional Abduction

13746637R00128

Made in the USA
Lexington, KY
18 February 2012